AVALON
QUEST FOR MAGIC

BOOK 4

The Heart of AvAlon

by Rachel Roberts

Other books in the Avalon series by Rachel Roberts

QUEST FOR MAGIC

BOOK 4

The Heart of AvAlon

by Rachel Roberts

red sky
publishing

CDS Books
New York

For information please address:

CDS Books
425 Madison Avenue
New York, NY 10017

ISBN: 1-59315-013-X

Orders, inquiries, and correspondence should be addressed to:

CDS Books
425 Madison Avenue
New York, NY 10017
(212) 223-2969, Fax (212) 223-1504

Printed in the United States of America

10   9   8   7   6   5   4   3   2   1

THE WORLD OF AVALON

❀ ❀ ❀ ❀ ❀ ❀ ❀ ❀ ❀ ❀

The Mages:

Emily
The healer, wears the rainbow jewel

Adriane
The warrior, wears the wolf stone

Kara
The blazing star, wears the unicorn jewel

Ozzie
An elf trapped in the body of a ferret, wears the ferret stone

Three teenagers and a ferret whose lives crisscross at the intersection of magic and friendship. Together they fight the dark powers bent on controlling the home of all magic, a mystical place called Avalon.

Magical Animal Friends:

Lyra
Winged leopard cat bonded to Kara

Dreamer
Mistwolf paladin bonded to Adriane

Stormbringer
Mistwolf bonded to Adriane

Ariel
Magical owl

Starfire
Fire stallion paladin bonded to Kara

The Drake
Dragon bonded to Zach and Adriane

❀ ❀ ❀ ❀ ❀ ❀ ❀ ❀ ❀ ❀

❁ ❁ ❁ ❁ ❁ ❁ ❁ ❁ ❁ ❁

Aldenmor:

Fairimentals	Protectors of the magic of Aldenmor, take form in different elements
Zach	A teenage boy raised by mistwolves, wears the dragon stone
Lorren	Goblin prince
Tasha	Goblin court sorceress

Home Base:
The Ravenswood Animal Preserve

The Dark Mages:

The Spider Witch	Elemental magic master
The Dark Sorceress	Half human, half animal magic user

The Quest:
Return nine missing power crystals to Avalon. Without these crystals, the magical secrets of Avalon will be lost forever.

❁ ❁ ❁ ❁ ❁ ❁ ❁ ❁ ❁ ❁

Ice Islands

Frozen Tundra

Mountains of Glass

Fairy Glade

Aquatania

Gnome Home

Mooregroves

The Anvil

Dream Lake

Cimarron Plains

Farthingdale

Mt. Hope

Misty Marshes

The Garden

Dumbledowns

Arahoo Wells

The Hook

Silver Forest

Wizards Crossing

Boggle Bog

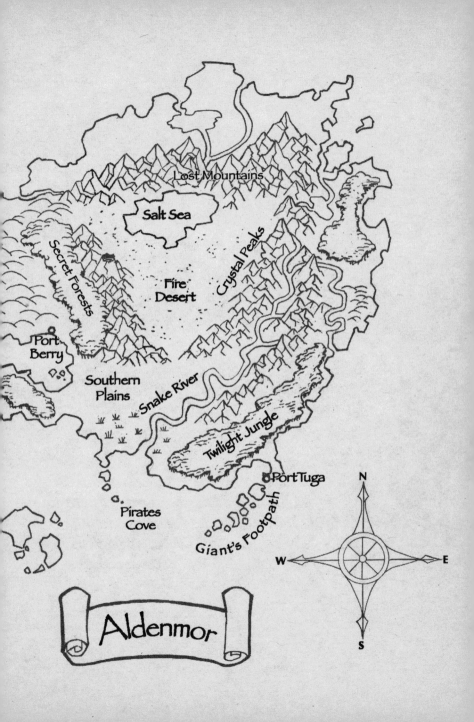

Lost Mountains

Salt Sea

Secret Forests

Crystal Peaks

Fire
Desert

Port
Berry

Southern
Plains

Snake River

Twilight Jungle

Port Tuga

Pirates
Cove

Giant's Footpath

N

W   E

S

Aldenmor

Chapter 1

"This place sure has changed," noted the golden brown ferret as he ran a paw through his static-charged cowlick.

"Are we even in the same place?" Emily Fletcher had to blink, she was so stunned.

What had once been a desolate wasteland known as the Shadowlands had turned into an enchanted paradise. She and Ozzie were in a beautiful garden, on a polished stone pathway surrounded by vibrant trees and sweet-smelling flowers. Behind them, the tall, silver mirror they had traveled through shimmered with magic.

Emily toyed with the blue and green jewel fastened to her bracelet and smiled.

If you had told her a year ago that she would become a mage and travel to different worlds using magic, she would have laughed out loud.

Emily had arrived in Stonehill, Pennsylvania, a year ago, the newcomer, friendless, and still hurting from her parents' divorce. In that short time, she had found Adriane Charday and Kara Davies—also thirteen years old—and one special friend, Ozzie, who was in a class all by himself. Ozzie was really an elf disguised as a ferret sent to earth from this world, Aldenmor, to find three mages. He looked like an ordinary ferret and for all intents, he *was* a ferret—that is, if your ferret happens to walk, talk, and make chocolate-chip pancakes.

Each mage had a different power, they'd discovered. Emily was the healer. Along with the warrior, Adriane, and the blazing star, Kara, it was their job to protect and preserve magic and all the creatures that depended on it.

She should have been feeling the joy of belonging. She was on a team, an important part of a secret club. But a familiar worry shadowed Emily's happiness. Kara and Adriane were far beyond her—they were both Level Two mages with paladins, powerful elemental protectors. And despite all she'd been through, Emily was still Level One. She hadn't even bonded with an animal yet—a vital part of advancing in magic. Ozzie helped her, but he'd turned out to be a unique mage, not the magical, bonded animal she needed.

A roar of commotion drifted over the trees.

Ozzie pointed. "Come on."

Emily followed the ferret down a hill and into a bustling field.

A pair of volcano-like structures covered in scaffolding rose from one end of an open courtyard.

Emily recognized them immediately. She shuddered at the remnants of the Dark Sorceress's lair. The half-human, half-animal magic master had once ruled the Shadowlands, releasing poisonous Black Fire that had devastated the land.

Now, as they looked on, hundreds of workers were building the foundations of a magnificent new city that would be home to all sorts of amazing species.

"Hey, watch the fur!" Ozzie bristled as a posse of excited pixies buzzed by.

A cluster of creatures crowded into the courtyard: burly dwarves, green-skinned goblins, wiry spriggans, and a host of others. Silver coins and carved amulets changed hands furiously. A bright flash caught her eye, and she gasped.

An immense troll, easily seven feet tall, roared from the center of the crowd. One massive hand wielded a heavy ax, the other a shield of wood and steel. Huge teeth curved from his mouth as the monster bellowed, "Who dares to challenge me?"

"GaH!" Ozzie leaped into Emily's arms to protect her from any sudden attack.

A tall girl stepped forward fearlessly. Long black hair pulled tight in a ponytail, she wore low-rise jeans, a black pullover, and a black down vest. On her wrist blazed a warrior's jewel, the wolf stone.

Assuming a fighting stance, Adriane Charday called out, "Let's see what you got."

"It's some kind of contest," Emily said.

With a roar, the troll thundered across the grassy ground, ax swinging.

A shield of light erupted from Adriane's jewel, deflecting the blow. The troll struck wide, burying the blade into the ground. Bellowing rage, the monster charged again.

Sidestepping easily, Adriane twisted the shield into a band of silver fire and whipped it around the troll's leg. Pulling tight, she sent the creature crashing to the ground. From out of thin air, a large black wolf appeared at the monster's throat, teeth bared and snarling.

The surprised troll let his ax fall to the ground. "I give!"

Cheers as well as groans went up from the crowd as the winners claimed their prizes.

Adriane extended her hand, helping the troll to his feet. She stepped back and bowed graciously.

"You are good—for a *human*," the troll rumbled.

"Thank you," she said, and smiled. "You honor me."

"Okay, break's over," a frazzled dwarf shouted. "Back to work!"

"Show-off." Emily approached her friend.

"Hey." Adriane grinned, retrieving her backpack from the sidelines. "I couldn't back down from a challenge. First impressions are everything, you know."

"Poor troll didn't have a chance, did he, Dreamer?" Emily knelt and ruffled the mistwolf's silky black coat.

"The bigger they are, the better they taste," Dreamer answered telepathically, lips pulled back in a wolfish grin.

"That Dark Sorceress had awful taste!"

The blazing star sauntered out the main gate of the structures. "You need some color in there."

Dressed in jeans, a lavender tee, and beige riding jacket with a fake-fur collar, the blond teen looked radiant, as usual. Her outfit was perfectly complemented by a pink, red, and white unicorn jewel dangling from a silver necklace.

A leopard-spotted cat padded beside her, Kara's bonded animal.

"I prefer the blue floral motif myself," Lyra suggested, long tail swishing.

A pretty teenage goblin girl trailed behind, her long moon-and-star-covered robes billowing. Her dark eyes were glued to a handheld device. "Ooo, I know a great fabric store in Lakeshire—everything we need for rugs and curtains."

Tasha had been appointed Court Sorceress for the Goblin Kingdom after her former boss, Tangoo, an evil magician, got tossed into the Otherworlds by Kara. The goblin girl had pale green skin, cute pointy ears, and short jet-black hair. She wore blue jeans and a bright red tee under her velvet robe.

"Hey, guys," Kara greeted them. "Emily, we thought you got lost."

"Sorry. Hi, Tasha." Emily gave the goblin girl a hug. Only an hour ago, she'd been in Stonehill, working at the Ravenswood Preserve. Tasha had magically transported her here, to the former Shadowlands.

The mages were on a quest to secure nine missing crystals of powerful magic before the evil sorceress and her ally, the Spider Witch, got them first. They had five remaining power crystals to find and no idea where they might be.

"The Fairimentals wanted you here fast, so I had to connect the Ravenswood portal directly to a mirror." Tasha led the group through the construction. "Hope the ride wasn't too bumpy."

The mages had been summoned by the Fairimentals, wondrous beings who protected Aldenmor, a world where magic still survived. The Fairimentals had renamed the sorceress's old lair The Garden and were turning it into a magic research center and school for mages.

"We're fine. My jewel just isn't as powerful as Adriane's or Kara's." The healer self-consciously tugged her jean jacket sleeve over her bracelet.

Tasha raised an eyebrow at Ozzie. "I guess your jewel hasn't changed yet, either?"

The ferret shook his head, adjusting the golden stone secured to his leather collar. "We're both still Level One."

"Tasha, what is that?" Emily asked, motioning toward the goblin girl's handheld device, which looked like a Sidekick.

"It's my jewel locator." She displayed her blinking device. "Cool, huh?"

"Another invention, eh? How does it work?" Ozzie asked.

Tasha brushed her bangs off her forehead. "Every jewel has a unique musical frequency. This device identifies and magnifies them. The stronger the jewel, the louder the tones."

Squeek! Rrrrrblat.

Kara and Adriane's jewels squawked and squealed as Tasha switched on the locator.

"Hellooo." The blazing star waved her twinkling unicorn jewel. "How come mine sounds horrible?"

"The unicorn jewel and the wolf stone emit completely opposite frequencies." Tasha indicated the modulating wave patterns on the small screen.

"Big surprise," Adriane scoffed.

"*Yours* is out of tune," Kara argued, turning her jewel between perfectly polished nails.

"Is not!" Adriane shook a burst of dazzling silver sparkles from her wolf stone. "You have no rhythm."

Emily spoke up quickly. "Can you find the others with that?"

"Well, theoretically," Tasha said, nodding. "But the missing power crystals are floating out there with wild magic. They have nothing to balance them."

"You mean like we have," Kara said, patting Lyra.

"Precisely. That's what makes you so powerful," Tasha continued.

"This one is stable now." Adriane held out her glowing backpack. Safe inside was a power crystal of Avalon, retrieved from the mistwolf Spirit Trail.

Tasha's eyes went wide. "I can't believe the Dark Sorceress just handed it to you."

Adriane shrugged. "The mistwolf spirit pack was inside it. Maybe she couldn't use it."

Tasha raised a finger thoughtfully. "I have a theory that power crystals are related to specific magic. This one fits the profile."

"The first one we found followed the unicorns to New Mexico," Kara mused.

"The power crystals are highly volatile," Tasha continued. "Yet they are stable in your hands."

"You mean because they were found by Adriane and Kara," Ozzie said.

"Yes, tuned to the magic of unicorns and mist-wolves, two of the most powerful of magical creatures." Tasha's ears wiggled in concentration. "Unless a power crystal bonds like those did, I can't get a stable reading."

The healer twisted at her silver bracelet. Kara and Adriane had only been Level One mages when they each recovered a power crystal, but Dreamer and Lyra had been at their sides. How was she supposed to do her part with no bonded animal to help her?

"Where should we put the one I have?" Adriane asked.

"We've converted that into a vault," Tasha said, proudly pointing to the sorceress's old lair.

"I thought those were destroyed," the warrior said uneasily, eyeing the glittering crystals poking through the top of the scaffolding.

Dreamer growled, his black hackles rising. The Dark Sorceress had trapped the mistwolves inside a giant crystal, trying to drain the pack's magic. She had nearly killed them all.

"That's the Crystal Keep now," Tasha explained. "Designed for the study of magic jewels."

"Tasha, you rock!" Kara exclaimed.

"Actually, I crystallize, Princess," the goblin girl answered as they followed a path of gleaming river stones into the heart of The Garden.

New trees stretched as far as the eye could see, growing into magnificent forests. A clear lake sparkled where a scorched desert once lay.

Tasha briskly turned down an adjoining path lined with foxgloves and primroses. Along the lakeshore sat pens filled with baby brimbees, wommels, pooxims, eqqtars, and some creatures Emily had never seen before.

"The Garden is an animal sanctuary, as well as a magic research center," Tasha informed them as the magical creatures swarmed after the mages.

The last time Emily had been on Aldenmor, she had healed dozens of animals injured by the Black Fire. Now all she sensed was the happiness they felt at having a new home. With a whole preserve full of animals, there must be one who would want to bond with her.

Thick bushes behind them rustled, revealing a group of glinting eyes. Several fuzzy kittens stepped forward cautiously, fur shimmering with orange, gold, silver, and black.

The cats swarmed around Kara, eager to get near the blazing star and her shining magic.

"They are orphans," Lyra said, licking down the ruff of a long-haired, white-and-silver-striped kitten.

"There's plenty of me for everyone." Kara giggled, petting the bouncing creatures.

Emily smiled, remembering how Kara had freaked out the first time magical animals had showered her with attention. Watching the blond girl bask in the adoration of the kittens, Emily stood to the side waiting for one to come to her.

What would it be like to have someone you could depend on all the time, the way Kara and Lyra, and Adriane and Dreamer supported each other? A perfect balance. No wonder Adriane and Kara were so far past her in their magic.

"Wait till you see this!" Tasha led the group around a thick grove of trees. Nestled in a beautiful meadow was a fantastic amphitheater with coils of yellow and red flowers laced through the wooden framework. Inside, rows of benches and toadstool seats had been meticulously constructed.

"Awesome!" Adriane declared, walking through the flowery archway.

"A gift from the Fairy Queen," Tasha explained proudly. "Imported piece by piece and supervised personally by—"

"Lorren!" Kara ran toward a cute goblin boy with spiky black hair and pale green skin. She had met the dashing Goblin Prince when she visited his home in the Fairy Realms.

He was setting up a tall mirror along with a blond teenage boy.

"Princess." Lorren grinned as he and Zach gently placed the mirror in a sculpted metal stand.

Kara smiled her million-dollar blazing star smile.

"Hi, Zach," Adriane said, beaming at the cute blond boy. The only human, as far as they knew, who lived on Aldenmor, Zach had been raised by the mist-wolves.

"Hi, Adriane."

The four of them stood like statues, staring into one another's eyes with silly grins.

Emily shifted uncomfortably. "This place is amazing."

"Oh, hey Emily, Ozzie," Zach greeted them warmly.

"Um . . . check out Tasha's new mirror," Lorren said.

"Quicksilver-edged coating for improved magical dispersion." Tasha beamed, looking over the installation.

"Uh . . . cool." Kara smiled encouragingly.

A brisk breeze blew Emily's red hair across her face.

Sparkles of light suddenly appeared in the center of the ring. Grass, leaves, and petals swirled together, forming a tumbleweed figure composed of earthly matter.

"Welcome, mages," Gwigg greeted in his gravelly voice.

"Gwigg, you old twig!" Ozzie ran to the earth Fairimental, sticking some extra flowers in place.

The Fairimental's large quartz eyes glimmered in the sunlight. "Sir Ozymandias, you are looking extra fuzzy."

"And whose fault is that?"

"We love it here," Kara said.

The air twinkled with magic as a second Fairimental took form, a translucent figure floating in the gentle breeze.

"The seeds of this beautiful place were planted when you released the magic of Avalon," Ambia, the air Fairimental, said in a lilting voice. Prisms of color danced along her shifting form. "But that magic now runs wild and could be used to strengthen our web— or destroy it."

Gwigg rumbled in agreement. "Even now, the Spider Witch is attempting to reweave the magic web. If enough of her web is completed, all the magic will be attracted to the new weaving. The magic of Avalon will be hers to control."

"You must save the home of all magic," Ambia concluded.

"But *we* don't know where Avalon is, exactly," Kara pointed out.

"We believe the nine power crystals will lead you to Avalon," Gwigg explained. "You must find them or all we have fought for will be lost."

"Once we get the rest of the crystals, what do we do with them?" Emily wondered.

"And what about the crystal that you-know-who"—Adriane nodded at the blazing star—"lost?"

Kara bristled. She had accidentally destroyed one of the crystals in the Fairy Realms.

"You must trust in the magic," Ambia said gently.

Emily stepped close to the Fairimentals. "How do *I* get to Level Two so I can better help my friends? I don't want to be left behind."

"Magic is all around you, young mage. Let it evolve in its own way," Gwigg said, as if that explained everything.

But what if mine never does? Emily wanted to wail. As a healer she couldn't practice her magic unless an animal was hurt—and that was the last thing she wanted. How was she supposed to catch up to her friends—wait around for some poor animal to get injured?

"Where do we look next?" Ozzie asked.

"There is a power crystal somewhere here on Aldenmor," Gwigg announced.

"Where?" Adriane asked.

"We don't know," Ambia continued. "Marina discovered it."

"Why not just ask her, then?" Emily suddenly realized that the water Fairimental had not joined them.

"Because Marina is missing," Gwigg rumbled ominously.

A Fairimental missing? This couldn't be good.

"Hey! Is this working?" A frantic voice suddenly filled the Fairy Ring.

The surface of the mirror flickered like television static.

"Yes, Marlin," Zach said, rolling his eyes. "What is it now?"

Tasha adjusted the mirror until the image sharpened. A boy about their age looked out, brown eyes wide with panic in his handsome, pale green face. His light brown hair had a lime tint, set off by the jewel-studded silver robes he wore.

"You must come right away!" He waved his arms in a clanking of rings and armbands. "The sea dragons are ruining the Wave Fest!"

"Prince Marlin, you are using unauthorized mirror transmissions," Tasha scolded.

"This is the most important thing going on in Aldenmor," Marlin said incredulously. "Attend me on the royal beach in five minutes. That's an order!"

The mirror abruptly went blank.

"What's his deal?" Adriane asked.

"That's the merprince of Aquatania," Zach explained. "It's a water city on the northern coasts of Aldenmor."

"He's also a spoiled snob," Lorren added. "He thinks these mirrors are his own personal line to the Fairimentals."

"The royal merfolk are fighting with the sea dragon riders," Zach continued. "The royals are turning away from magic and claim the riders only care about themselves."

"I'm friends with several dragon riders and their sea dragons," Adriane protested. "They're not like that at all."

Zach nodded. "The Wave Fest is a goodwill party for the two groups to reconcile."

"I'll go," Emily volunteered. At last, there was something she could do.

Everyone stared at the healer.

She shrugged. "Maybe I can help out with the sea dragons."

"We'll join you as soon as we get the power crystal

back to the Keep," Tasha said, and nodded. "I also want to scan the princess's and Adriane's jewels."

"That okay, Emily?" Adriane asked, taking Zach's hand.

"Sure, Ozzie and I will call if we need anything."

"The mirror should take you right there." Lorren bowed to Emily, gesturing to the flat, glimmering surface. "All you have to do is step through."

"Let's go," Ozzie said.

"Later, 'gators," Kara said, and waved.

Taking a deep breath, Emily closed her eyes and plunged through the mirror. It was like passing through a thin layer of chill water. She stepped out, gasping as dizzying waves of magic washed over her. Someone was in terrible pain.

Chapter 2

Emily found herself on a rocky beach in the middle of a magical carnival.

All types of creatures from Aldenmor—mermaids and merboys, elves, goblins, dwarves, fairies, and spriggans—were enjoying the Wave Fest despite the gray skies. A giant octopus Oct-A-Whirl tossed seashells full of merchildren in the air. Their delighted whoops of joy almost drowned out the buzz coming from dozens of brightly decorated stalls lining the beach.

Just offshore, a sprawling city of huge translucent bubbles rose from the aquamarine surf.

Behind Emily, the mirror bent and remolded itself around Ozzie's body as he stepped through. "Wow, Aquatania," he marveled.

"Ouch!" Pain pulsed up Emily's arm as a spray of purple sparks burst from her jewel.

"What?" Concern furrowed Ozzie's furry brow.

"Someone's hurt."

The ferret jumped to attention, scanning the crowds. "Over there."

Down the beach, a group of mergirls and boys were facing off with the same merprince who'd spoken through the mirror. His elaborate silver robes and jewelry sparkled in the sun.

"Your dragons are ruining everything!" the merprince bellowed.

"Oh, no!" Emily gasped. Dozens of huge green, purple, and blue sea dragons lay motionless in the surf. Waves lapped over their iridescent scales, tugging long, coiled tails back and forth in the tide. "Let's go, Ozzie."

"Call off the Wave Fest!" A tall merboy wearing a shiny green and blue body suit was in the merprince's face, his sea blue eyes flashing with worry and anger. "These dragons are sick."

"Well, get them back in the water," the prince retorted.

"They shouldn't be moved." Emily stepped forward self-consciously.

The bejeweled merprince faced Emily and Ozzie. "Who are you?"

"I'm Emily, a healer. And this is Ozzie."

The merprince scowled at Ozzie. "I asked for a Fairimental, not a *furry*mental."

"gAh!" Ozzie bristled, his fur ruffling. "I'm a mage!"

The tall merboy who'd been at odds with the merprince shook Emily's hand. "I am Jaaran." He motioned to the other merteens. All wore sparkling star-shaped jewels on bracelets or necklaces. "These are the dragon riders of Aquatania."

Emily felt their anguish and fear for their bonded sea dragons.

"I'm Ozzie of Farthingdale." Ozzie puffed out his furry chest and waggled his magic jewel. "Perhaps you've heard of it."

The loud merprince pushed in front of Emily. "*I* am Prince Marlin."

"She's the healer mage!" A mergirl with green skin and hair braided with glittering pearls sat on the surf's edge. She gently stroked her sea dragon's horse-like head as the creature whined softly, its large golden eyes dull and glassy. "I'm Kee-lyn."

Emily marveled at the dragons. They were incredible creatures with long, sleek bodies and wide aerodynamic fins built for speed. Powerful hind legs could propel them through the rough waters of the oceans while shorter forelegs were used for balance.

"You. Healer. Fix these dragons before the Wave Fest is completely ruined," the prince commanded.

"Give her some room," Ozzie ordered.

Emily knelt beside Kee-lyn's dragon.

"I'm Emily," she said softly to the animal. "What's your name?"

"*Meerka.*" The dragon's voice echoed weakly in her mind. "*The warrior mage is my friend.*"

"Mine too." Emily smiled. Setting her backpack down in the sand, she patted the dragon and took a deep breath. "Easy, Meerka. I won't hurt you."

Holding up her rainbow jewel, Emily placed her hand on Meerka's neck. The dragon's smooth scales felt slightly warm.

"Ozzie."

The ferret was at the healer's side instantly, orange stone glowing as he added his magic to hers.

The healer opened her senses, trying to feel what Meerka felt. The dragon's heart thrummed with a weak but steady pulse as Emily searched for any wounds, cuts, or broken bones.

Physically, Meerka seemed okay. But something was making the dragon sick. Emily pushed deeper, trying to find the source of the illness. Tendrils like fine silk brushed her mind. The dragon's magic flickered like a weak flame, threatening to extinguish with each breath. Something was eating away at Meerka's magic like a virus!

Emily sent glowing blue and green healing light cascading over the dragon's immense body. She visualized the animal becoming healthy, picturing the strong muscles and bright, colorful scales.

Her rainbow jewel sparked with an electrical charge.

Emily recoiled in fear as the dragon groaned painfully.

"Emily." Ozzie's concerned voice grounded the healer.

"It's okay." Emily stroked Meerka's head soothingly, feeling increasingly nervous.

She'd healed many kinds of injuries, but this was completely different. The sickness eating away at Meerka was something she had never encountered before. She had no clue how to put the deteriorating magic back together. Was healing Meerka simply beyond her Level One skills?

She sat back and sighed, trying not to let the dragon riders see her worry. Unless Emily learned how to cure Meerka, all the sea dragons could lose their magic.

Get a grip, she scolded herself. Kara and Adriane would be here soon to help.

"Good. All fixed. Let's go," Prince Marlin ordered.

"It's not all fixed," Emily said tersely. "The dragons have to stay here and rest."

"They're blocking the goodwill ceremony!" The prince tapped his royal foot impatiently.

"Do you have any idea what made them sick?" Emily asked.

"Magic," Marlin spat, and gestured offshore.

Emily's attention was drawn to a brightly colored splash on the horizon, like fireworks in the middle of the day. "What is that?"

"The wild magic storm cloud," Marlin informed

her. "It's all those sea dragons' fault! Magic attracts magic. Everyone knows that."

"What does a jerk attract?" Jaaran yelled.

"Where are the rest of your dragons?" Emily asked, scanning the large group of riders.

"There are no more," a merboy said sadly.

"Since the Dark Sorceress hunted so many, very few dragon riders even *have* bonded dragons." Jaaran sighed. "These are the last of the sea dragons."

Emily's heart went out to them. So many riders and no dragons to bond with.

"You can heal them, right?" Kee-lyn implored, holding Meerka tight.

Emily hesitated, but she couldn't lie to the dragon riders.

"I'm not sure. If we can't find a treatment . . . they could lose their magic."

"Proves everything I've been saying for months." Marlin crossed his arms. "The time of magic is over."

"What about the pups?" another rider asked.

"Pups?" Ozzie asked.

"The dragon babies."

"Take me to them." Emily anxiously slipped the straps of her backpack over her shoulders.

"Over here." Jaaran hurried around a jagged rock outcropping.

"I have to prepare my speech," the merprince grumbled as he followed.

Emily glared at him as she pulled her jacket tight

against the sharp winds whistling through the high cliff walls.

But the healer forgot all about Marlin when she saw the pups. The plump, seal-like babies huddled together, trembling, golden eyes wide with fear. Their soft, scaly bodies ranged from pearly pale blues to deep emerald greens.

Emily knelt beside the closest pup. Power suddenly gathered in her jewel, tingling up and down her arm.

"BlaaHHH!"

Pups rolled across the sand as a purple blur erupted from the center of the pile.

A pink and purple dragon, larger than the others, barreled toward Emily, its deep blue eyes gleaming.

"Who are you?" Ozzie eyed the strange creature suspiciously.

"Ooooooo." The pup reached for Ozzie's jewel.

"Hey, don't touch the ferret!" Ozzie yelped.

"Schmootek!" The purple pup shoved the ferret aside, its wide mouth open in a toothy grin as it scampered up to the healer.

"Hi, there." Emily reached down and patted this odd dragon.

"Blooop." The creature's wide face crumpled into a pathetic grimace. He pointed at his big toe and whimpered, shining blue eyes locked on the rainbow jewel.

"All right, let's take a look at you."

The creature sat on its rump, wide feet splayed. Its skin was smooth, and instead of fins, it had big—toes!

"You don't look like a sea dragon." Brushing red curls from her face, she picked up a foot and inspected it.

The creature eyed her jewel intently.

Emily felt his soft neck, trying to find his pulse. Nothing. She couldn't feel a thing! The pup stared up at her with glinting blue eyes, his chest rising and falling with each breath. Maybe I'm just really tired, she thought.

"What's wrong, Emily?" Ozzie asked.

"I don't know." The healer swallowed, her throat closing in panic. Her rainbow gem wasn't picking up anything. What if she'd lost her healing magic altogether?

"Beebee!" The creature suddenly leaped into Emily's lap and grabbed at her jewel with lumpy fingers.

"Get away from her!" Ozzie yelled, prying the creature away.

"Haka!" Purple lips stretched wide, the plump dragon suddenly let go and ran away.

At the same exact moment, thunder crashed overhead as flecks of light sparkled in the clouds.

The rainbow stone pulsed deeply, sending a prickling up Emily's arm. Danger!

Screaming erupted from the beach. But Emily's

eyes were locked on the dazzling lights twisting from the dark, billowing clouds.

"Oh no!" Ozzie screamed.

They had seen these before. Tornadoes of wild magic. She and Adriane had been caught in one, and it had temporarily played havoc with their magic. Even Ozzie had been transformed.

Scrambling around the dunes, she saw several cyclones whirl across the beach.

"Stay out of their way!" Emily screamed at the crowds running for cover.

Spirals of orange, silver, red, and blue advanced dangerously, digging deep trenches in the sand, tearing into food stands and overturning the Oct-A-Whirl. And in the middle of the chaos, the purple and pink sea dragon shimmied and shook, attracting the twisters like bees to honey.

"What is that?" Prince Marlin demanded, pointing to the dancing purple creature.

"It's your ocean," Emily said.

Barreling through the crowded carnival, the baby dragon sent pixies and elves flying—the tornadoes chasing after him.

Jaaran and the dragon riders circled their dragons, star-shaped jewels crackling with power as they formed a pearly protective shield.

"Emily, watch out!" Ozzie yelled, pointing over her shoulder.

The purple and pink sea dragon was racing

straight for her, mouth opened, tongue waggling—three sparkling twisters bearing down behind him.

"Beebee!"

"Emily!" Ozzie stepped in front of the healer.

"Ozzie!" Emily reached out. But the sea dragon smacked straight into the ferret.

"Ahhh!" Ozzie tumbled head over tail as the twisters engulfed him. Trapped in the swirling wild magic, the brave ferret was swept into the air.

The sky overhead suddenly disappeared in a funnel of swirling colors. Caught in the full force of the churning magic, Emily took one last gulp of air as the world flashed brilliant white.

Chapter 3

Something gritty rubbed against Emily's cheek. A soft rushing noise filled her ears as she pushed herself up on her elbows, wiping sand and wet hair from her face.

She was lying in the surf, the tide gently lapping at her feet. Struggling to stand, she shielded her eyes from the sharp glare of a glittering turquoise ocean. Patterns of bright light twinkled across the azure surface.

"Ozzie?" She whirled around in panic. "Where are you?"

A sparkling white beach curved out of sight in both directions. Palm trees covered her in swaying shadows. She seemed to be on a tropical island. It didn't look a thing like the rocky beach of Aquatania.

But how had she ended up here—wherever *here* was?

Emily could make out a coastline of rolling hills across the wide expanse of water. Wispy puffs of white smoke rose into the sky.

"Hey!" She waved her hands until she realized no one could see her.

Raising her rainbow jewel, she sent blue-green sparkles twinkling in the air. "Ozzie? Come in, Ozzie!" she called. "Doc Doolittle to Fuzzy One."

Silence.

"Adriane? Kara?" She paused, her pulse pounding in her ears. "Lyra, Dreamer, anybody?"

Willing the magic to reach her friends, Emily sent a beam of jewel light swirling toward the sky. Abruptly the light splintered with a ringing sound. A faint shield shimmered overhead like a mirage.

"What's going on?" With a trembling hand she brushed tangled hair out of her face.

Turning, she tried another angle. But no matter where she aimed her magic, an intense, hazy shimmer blocked it.

The entire place seemed to be enveloped in a magic shield.

No reason to panic, she told herself, scanning the dense jungle vegetation shrouding the island's interior. Kee-lyn and Jaaran were probably looking for her, and Kara, Adriane, and her other friends would be arriving at the Wave Fest any minute now. But she knew she was nowhere near the blustery waters and towering cliffs of Aquatania.

Looking out at the glittering sea, she felt her hopes sinking below the surface. Was she really stranded on a strange island, totally alone?

Emily sloshed up the beach and swung off her backpack. At least the pack had stayed with her the whole time.

She peeled off her denim jacket and set it on a piece of bleached driftwood. If only her rainbow stone was strong enough to make sure Ozzie was safe. This was the first time she could ever remember not being able to find him.

What if she was stranded on the island for days, or weeks? What would happen to the animals back home in Stonehill at the Pet Palace? Mom will take care of them, she thought, settling back down. But still . . . what if she couldn't get back? Her mom would totally freak!

A wet strand of hair dripped stinging salt water into her eyes. Sighing, she opened her backpack to get a scrunchy.

"Ozzie," she said, giggling. Inside was a soggy package of oatmeal cookies, a water bottle, turkey jerky, two PowerBars, a hat, sunscreen, a brush, two scrunchies, and a ferret comb. Yup, Ozzie had done the packing. What she wouldn't give to see that furry ferret standing there now.

"Always looking out for me." She smiled.

"rrrrmmmmm."

A strange, low growl emanated from the depths of the tropical jungle. Emily swung around, jewel raised. "Who's there?"

A shadow bolted between thick palm trees.

Squinty eyes peered at her from behind wide, fringed leaves.

"You'd better not try anything!" She hoped she sounded calm. A wild animal would be able to read the emotions in her voice.

But the creature who staggered from the jungle onto the beach was small and familiar.

"Ozzie!" Emily exclaimed, running forward.

"Beebee!"

Emily grabbed the ferret in a huge hug, burying her face in his fur. He was slightly sticky and smelled like sea salt. The ferret pushed away, landed on his rump, and sat there, big eyes blinking.

"Oh, I was so worried!" She pulled back and studied Ozzie. He looked all right—except his normally gold and brown fur was purple and pink!

"Ozzie?"

"Beebee?"

"What happened to you?"

"Soda." The ferret turned and grabbed Emily's backpack.

Oh, no! The last time Ozzie had been caught in a wild magical whirlwind, his tail had been transformed into a beaver tail. This time—

"Blah-haha!" The purple ferret cackled gleefully as he turned her backpack upside down, dumping everything into his wide, toothy mouth.

"Glurp!" Ozzie chomped a pair of green socks with big square teeth.

"That's my ladybug sock!" Emily lunged for her stuff, playing tug-o-sock. "Spit it out!"

The ferret looked up at her, a stubborn expression on his face, and clamped his lips shut.

"Come on."

Ozzie shook his head from side to side.

Emily pounded him on the back, making him spit out the sock.

"Ppphllt!" Ozzie dove forward in the sand and began scooping PowerBars into his mouth, wrappers and all.

Even for the ever-hungry Ozzie, this was weird.

"Emmmeeemee."

"Huh?"

He sidled up to her with a bobbing walk that rocked from side to side almost like he wasn't used to legs. He stuck out a large lavender lip and pouted. Big blue eyes brimmed with tears as he fell back on his rump.

"What do you want now?"

Ozzie pointed to a stubby big toe. "Owwie."

"You're hurt?"

"Ahgaga!" He waved his hairy foot in her face, nodding emphatically.

"Sit still," Emily ordered. "I'll take a look."

Closing her eyes, Emily tried to form a connection. A wave of blackness washed over her, as if she'd suddenly gone blind. She couldn't feel anything at all. The same thing had happened when she tried to heal

31

that weird sea dragon pup at the Wave Fest. But this was *Ozzie*, her closest friend.

Then she froze as she saw Ozzie's neck—there was no collar. "Ozzie, what happened to your ferret stone?"

Ozzie sat in the sand gnawing on the straps of her backpack.

"Spitooie!" Wide indigo eyes locked on her rainbow jewel. "Oooooo."

Realization dawned.

"You're not Ozzie! Who are you? What happened to Ozzie?" The healer scrambled to her feet, but the creature was too fast for her. He grabbed her wrist, tugging at the bracelet that held her jewel.

"Ow!" Emily pulled back. "Stop it! You're hurting me!"

Wild colors swirled across her jewel's surface, racing up her arm. A burst of power sent the creature tumbling back.

Something twinkled in his small paw.

"No." Emily held up her wrist, panicked. Her healing stone was no longer on her silver bracelet.

"A har!"

Emily watched, horrified, as the purple creature tossed the jewel in his mouth and swallowed with a strangled gulp.

"Ahhhhhh," he said with a satisfied grin.

"No!"

"Blah ha ha!" The creature jumped to his feet, hopped about, and barreled into the tropical jungle.

"Come back here!" Emily screamed.

But it was too late. The purple and pink *whatever it was*—and her healing stone—were gone!

❧ ❧ ❧

"What rained on this parade?" Kara surveyed the overturned Oct-A-Whirl and crushed food stalls littering the Wave Fest.

Beached sea dragons sprawled across the shore, surrounded by angry merfolk. The prince's guards swarmed around the dragons, fencing off the surrounding beach. Barges floated offshore, confining the dragons to a small area of water.

Tasha's jewel device beeped as she walked through the debris.

Dreamer padded over to Adriane. *"There has been a lot of magical activity here."*

Lyra landed, her golden wings folding and disappearing. *"I can't reach Emily or Ozzie."*

The blazing star clutched her unicorn jewel, frowning. "Me either."

Adriane and Kara exchanged a worried glance.

"Those are the dragon riders," Zach said, pointing to the group of tough-looking warriors. "We don't want to mess with those guys."

"Jaaran!" Adriane ran to the tall sea dragon rider and gave him a hug.

"Adriane, I'm so glad you're here."

Zach raised an eyebrow.

Lorren grinned. "Probably just friends, you know."

"Yeah, I can see that."

Adriane stepped back from Jaaran and flushed. "Jaaran, this is—"

"Yes, I've met Zach." Jaaran sized up the blond teen. "We have much in common."

They looked on as the dark-haired warrior hugged Kee-lyn and Meerka.

"We both ride dragons," Jaaran said.

Zach nodded. "I'm sorry your dragons are not well."

"The healer was trying to help them," Kee-lyn explained.

"Where is she?" Adriane asked.

"Gone," a rider answered.

"What do you mean 'gone'?" Kara demanded.

"Aquatania is closed! Everyone go home!" shouted a merman with graying hair and beard. His purple ceremonial robes billowed as he stormed up and down the beach, golden crown gleaming atop his head.

"That's King Spartos," Lorren said.

"Your majesty." Kara pushed her way past the barricades. "I am the blazing star."

"You!" The king's sea green eyes angrily studied Adriane and Kara. "This whole mess is your fault."

"Go blazing diplomat," Adriane muttered.

"What happened here?" Kara pressed.

"My son is missing!" the king cried.

"Prince Marlin is gone, too?" Adriane asked.

The king flashed a dark look at Kee-lyn and Jaaran. "These dragon riders were the last ones to be seen with him."

"What are you insinuating?" Jaaran's cheeks flushed deep green.

"It's no secret you'd prefer a dragon rider as next king," Spartos accused.

Kara planted her hands on her hips. "Look, we don't have time to chitchat. Our friend is missing."

"So is our merprince!" the king bellowed.

"Well, so is our ferret!" Kara retorted.

The king bristled.

"Kara," Lorren said, pulling the blazing star back. "May I?"

Kara waved her hand forward. "Knock yourself out."

"King Spartos," Lorren approached the merking. "With all due respect, sir, the three mages saved Aldenmor."

The king grunted.

"The blazing star saved the Fairy Realms as well," Lorren acknowledged Kara.

"You are right, of course, young goblin prince." Spartos raised a bushy eyebrow at Kara. "I'm very upset."

"Apology accepted," Kara said, and smiled. "We'll

do everything we can to find your son and our friends."

"Very well." The tall merking sighed. "Let the mages investigate."

Lorren turned to Kara. "Well?"

"Impressive."

King Spartos looked sadly at the sea dragon warriors. "I am sorry, dragon riders. Once those dragons served us well. But I fear the time of magic is over."

"We will not let our dragons die!" proclaimed one of the riders. "They are the last of their kind! The last of *our* magic."

The king snorted, pointing to the messy beach. "And look what your magic did."

"We had nothing to do with that wild magic storm!" Jaaran insisted.

"Wait a minute, what wild magic?" Adriane asked.

"A wild magic storm swept through the Wave Fest moments before they disappeared," Jaaran explained. "No one has seen them since."

"I've got something," Tasha called out, eyes glued to her magic locator. "Portal residue."

"Eww." Kara checked her pink sneakers.

"Oops, sorry, Lyra." Tasha distractedly walked right into the big cat. "Emily definitely fell through a portal."

The goblin girl pushed some buttons on her machine. Light streamed upward, projecting a map of Aldenmor. Twinkling dots indicated portals. "I have a copy of Moonshadow's fairy map loaded in here."

"You can do that?" Kara asked.

"It's a crystal storage device harmonically tuned to—"

"Yeah, she can do that." Lorren smiled.

"Where is Emily now?" Zach asked.

"I don't know. According to the map, there's not supposed to be a portal here on Aquatania Beach."

Kara's face fell. "They could be anywhere."

"Like right here." Tasha adjusted a knob as the device squeaked.

"You found Emily's jewel?"

"I'm getting a fuzzy reading a few miles due south."

"Drake!" Zach called his bonded animal, who had flown from The Garden to Aquatania.

A massive red dragon soared from the skies, landing among the startled merfolk. Drake roared with distress as he saw his cousins, the sick sea dragons.

"Easy," Zach soothed his friend.

Adriane scratched behind the dragon's ear. "We're going to help them."

"Okay, Mama."

"He is amazing!" Impressed dragon riders gathered around the red Drake. "This is your dragon?"

"Yes," Adriane said, smiling proudly. "He imprinted on me, but Zach is his rider."

Two flying goblin bats swooped from the skies and landed next to Lorren and Tasha.

"Good girl, Gertie." A gray and white bat nuzzled Tasha as she hopped into the red leather saddle.

"Let's go!" Zach climbed into the black and tan saddle on Drake's back. He reached down to help Adriane aboard as Dreamer leaped behind her. The mistwolf settled into a basket secured to Drake's back.

"After you, Princess." Lorren helped Kara onto Nightwing, his black goblin bat.

"We'll find Marlin and Emily," Kara promised the dragon riders.

"And Ozzie," Lyra added.

"And bring back a cure for your dragons," Adriane said confidently.

With that, the flying foursome soared into the stormy clouds overhead.

Chapter 4

Emily trudged up an incline dotted with palm trees. She had to find the purple creature who'd eaten her jewel. She could not stop shivering as her emotions swung between anger and fear.

She looked at her empty bracelet. What would she do without her magic?

Maybe she was better off, she thought forlornly. A few hours ago she had been worried about becoming a Level Two mage. Now the sea dragons were about to become extinct, she was lost on some island, she had no idea where the real Ozzie was, and she had no jewel! Some mage she was turning out to be—

A piece of wood snapped.

Emily froze, trying to listen and look everywhere at once.

Warm winds sent glints of sunlight waving through the palms.

Another branch snapped loudly. Something was tromping through the underbrush, coming right toward her!

Emily whirled. Where could she hide? Her heart pounded in her throat. Without her jewel, she was completely defenseless.

"Baaaaah!" Branches flew as a figure sprang from the bushes. "Don't make me use this!"

"Marlin!" Emily cried with relief. "Is that a coconut?"

"*Prince* Marlin," the merboy corrected her, brandishing . . . yup, a coconut!

"You're the mage!" He pointed a bejeweled finger. "I won't tolerate being kidnapped."

"Kidnapped?" Emily echoed, astounded.

"You attracted wild magic and zapped us here."

"I don't know how we got here," the healer told him. "But I'm glad to see you."

"Me too, this was getting heavy." Marlin stepped back into the bushes and dragged out a palm frond filled with coconuts and brightly colored fruits. "Get these, will you? I'm exhausted."

The merprince strode down the dunes toward the beach, brushing off his bright ceremonial robe.

"Hey!" Emily grabbed the edges of the palm frond, straining to drag it across the hot sand. "Do you have any idea where we are?"

Marlin glanced at the two pale orbs just visible in the afternoon sky.

"Judging by the position of the moons, we're somewhere on the Giant's Footpath, a group of islands on the southeastern shore of Aldenmor. That must be Port Tuga over there."

Emily gazed at the landmass in the distance. "How do we get across?"

"Use your magic."

"I'm a healer, not a helicopter." She looked at her bare wrist. "Besides, my magic is gone."

"I'm not surprised. Magic has been vanishing for a while now."

"No, I mean my jewel—" The empty silver bracelet gleamed in the sunlight. "Oh, never mind."

"I'm hungry," the prince complained, stretching out on the sand, hands folded behind his head.

Emily dropped the leaf near her backpack. "How can you be so calm?"

"Relax. The Imperial Merfolk will find us."

"Well, you'll be waiting a long time." She fished a water bottle from her pack. "This island is hidden by a magic shield. I don't think anyone can see us."

"What did you do now?" Marlin demanded.

"I didn't do anything." Emily glared down at him.

"Why would someone put a shield around an island?"

"I don't know, but we're trapped here, and unless we get back soon, you're going to lose your dragons."

"The dragon riders have no place left in our society. The sooner they accept it, the better."

"There must be something you can do."

"Well, I know what *you* can do." Marlin leaned back against a piece of driftwood. "Fix me lunch."

Emily's jaw dropped. Who did this guy think he was?

"What? It's your fault we're here!" Marlin exclaimed. "Humans shouldn't be allowed to use magic—they always mess things up."

Emily gritted her teeth. "We must have fallen through a portal. But I didn't open it."

"You didn't?" Marlin looked up at her, brow wrinkling in confusion. "Well, if you didn't and I didn't, then who did?"

"I'm going to find out."

"Can we eat first?"

"Fine." Emily stood with her arms crossed. "Go right ahead."

"Fine!" Marlin leaned forward, arranging driftwood in a circle. "That's the trouble with magic: It's completely unreliable. When I'm king, Aquatania will be much better off without it."

"You can't be serious." Emily was shocked. "Dragons are your bonded animals."

"I don't need magical animals. I figure everything out right here." Marlin tapped his head with a piece of wood.

Emily couldn't believe his attitude. "These animals are essential for magic," she argued angrily.

"Oh? Where's your bonded animal?"

Emily's face fell. "I . . . don't have one."

"Uh-huh, and where's the magic on your world?"

Emily flushed. "Except for Ravenswood, I haven't technically seen any magic."

"I rest my case," Marlin huffed. "Aldenmor's going to be just like Earth. It's called evolution. The sooner we accept it, the better. Look at me," he said, proudly displaying a delicately webbed hand. "The perfected product of evolution."

"Your brain is so big, I'm surprised your head isn't gigantic. Oh, wait. It is!"

"That's not funny," he said, self-consciously patting down his poofy brown hair. "Besides, we don't have a choice, do we? No dragons, no magic."

Emily had never heard such stubborn arrogance in her life. "So use your advanced merbrain to get us out of here instead of sitting around complaining."

"All right, I will!" Marlin burst out, then shut his mouth with a snap. A dark green blush washed across his cheeks.

"Well, I'm waiting."

"Well, I'm thinking."

She slumped down beside the merprince, handing him the water bottle. "Great, we'll be here forever."

❧   ❧   ❧

Adriane tightened her grip around Zach's waist as Drake glided over the rough northern waters. Gertie and Nightwing flew side by side in front of the dragon, with Lyra in the lead, golden wings glimmering.

The warrior zipped her vest tight and glanced over her shoulder at Dreamer.

"What you got?"

Dreamer's head poked out of his basket, tongue lolling, fur blowing in the wind. *"I smell a ferret."*

Deep blue waters flashed beneath them, broken by jagged rocks that rose from the sea like monster's teeth.

"I can't see anything but water," Kara complained, scrunching behind Lorren to block the spray from her face.

"Coming up right on it," Tasha called. Her robes whipped behind her as she studied her magic meter.

Below them, bobbing in the choppy waves, a giant tortoise meandered its way between rocky islands off the shore. As big as the creature was, it looked teeny in the vastness of the ocean.

"Hurry up, you floating thing!" Ozzie jumped up and down on the tortoise's shell, making it rock precariously. "At this rate we'll get to Aquatania in a year!"

Skimming across the surf, the Drake landed with a belly flop.

A huge wave bounced the tortoise high in the air, washing it onto an outcropping of rocks. The dragon floated to a stop, nose to nose with the shocked tortoise and ferret.

"GahAhh! Don't eat me!"

"Ozzie, it's us," Adriane called down from the back of the dragon.

"Oh."

Drake's long, forked tongue shot out, lifting the ferret into the air and dropping him onto the dragon's head.

"Are you okay?" Adriane asked.

"Gak!" Ozzie wiped dragon slobber off his head. "I've been floating out here forever!"

"At least an hour," Zach observed.

"Exactly!" Ozzie looked up as the two giant bats landed on the rocks. "Where's Emily?"

"That's what we were going to ask you," Adriane said.

"I knew it!" Ozzie flapped his arms in the air. "She's been kidnapped! gaH!"

"What are you talking about?"

"That purple toothed, grin-eating farFOoFiE!" Ozzie screamed.

"Ozzie, calm down," Kara ordered. "Tell us what happened."

"These cyclones hit the beach. I went one way," he said, pointing. "Then Emily went the other way." He crossed his arms, pointing with his other paw. "Then that sea dragon went the other way!" He pointed with his foot and toppled over.

Zach grabbed him by the tail and swung him in the air. The ferret landed on Lyra's back.

"*Hi.*"

"Fine! Where were you?!"

"What sea dragon?" Adriane asked.

"This purple sea dragon attracted wild magic."

"That's weird," Tasha murmured, fine-tuning dials. "I'll say!"

"No, I mean for a second I thought I had a lock on Emily's jewel."

"Here, I'll give you a boost." Kara shot a fine beam of dazzling red and white magic into Tasha's device, as she bragged, "My jewel's the most powerful."

Adriane gave her a scowl. "*Mine* actually has some of Emily's magic in it." The warrior directed a steady silver beam to the other side of Tasha's jewel locator.

A piercing screech filled the air as wolf and unicorn magic collided, shattering in a flurry of sparks.

"No good." Tasha hurriedly pushed a button, cutting off the noise. "Your jewels are exact opposites. You can't work together without a balancing factor."

"What a surprise," Adriane muttered.

"Here, try this." Sunlight reflected through Ozzie's jewel as he sent a beam of his pure gold light across the magic meter.

This time, a set of croaking notes rang forth with no feedback.

"That's better." Tasha nodded in satisfaction.

Everyone leaned forward as blue and green lights swept back and forth on Tasha's small screen. Sparkles of purple and pink tinged the edges.

"Fascinating," Tasha said, adjusting the dials.

"What?" Ozzie asked.

"I've located Emily's jewel, but the signature is different." Tasha looked up.

"Is that good or bad?" Kara asked.

"Your jewels change as you become more powerful, but the core signature should never change. It's who you are. It's as if someone else is using her jewel."

"You sure it's hers?" Lorren asked.

"Quite," Tasha confirmed. "The readings are coming from somewhere in the southern islands."

"That's dangerous country," Zach said, frowning. "Mostly unexplored jungles."

"How long will it take us to get there?" Adriane asked.

"A few days, if we fly directly across the Moorgroves and over the Burning Deserts," Zach said.

The others groaned.

"We *could* try another way." Tasha held up the magic meter so everyone could see the blinking dots. "There's a series of four portals that crisscross Aldenmor."

"Jump the four at once," Adriane said, nodding.

"How?" Kara demanded.

"You'll have to make a rope out of magic," Tasha explained. "Anchoring it to Emily's jewel, we can slingshot through the four simultaneously."

"Tasha's a genius," Lorren said, beaming. "How many times have you done this?"

Tasha blinked. "Exactly none."

"Emily's all alone!" Ozzie cried, then his eyes opened wide. "Or not."

"I love portal hopping." Kara faced the warrior. "What do you think, Xena?"

"Okay, Barbie. Let's go for it."

The mages knocked fists, then turned to Ozzie. The ferret gave the girls a determined nod.

❧   ❧   ❧

The sun sank slowly toward the horizon, tingeing the ocean a beautiful pale pink. Emily dragged a piece of driftwood across the beach, heaving it onto the crackling fire Marlin had built.

"I didn't think a merprince like you would know anything about camping." Emily watched as the merboy poked at several rolled-up banana leaves filled with purple potatoes and fruits roasting on the coals.

"Of course I do," he answered. "I was in the merscouts."

Emily's mouth watered as smoke wafted into the air. She had forgotten how hungry she was. The last thing she'd eaten was a bowl of Cheerios at home in Stonehill that morning.

"Here." Marlin plopped a few steaming leaf bundles on a large abalone shell and handed it to Emily.

"You might be a snob, but you sure are resourceful." Emily smiled, taking a big bite of the hot fruit compote. Her eyes lit up. It was delicious.

Marlin watched her as she ate. "You never bonded

with an animal? I thought that's what mages were supposed to do: bond with animals and make magic to save the world."

Emily paused before responding. "I guess I haven't found my bonded yet."

"What about the weird ferret?"

"He's an elf and he's not weird!" Emily shot back, then relaxed. "My friends and I . . . we don't have any formal training or anything. We just try to do the best we can."

"But you still use magic without an animal." Marlin seemed fascinated with the concept.

"Yes. But I'm only a Level One mage. Kara and Adriane are Level Two."

Marlin chewed thoughtfully. "You know, once upon a time, merfolk were full of elemental magic. I mean we even had scales and tails! But we don't need magic anymore." His nose got higher in the air with every word. "As I said, we are evolving away from magic."

"In my world, so many species are lost every year because of 'evolution,'" Emily said. "And now your dragons might not make it. You're the merprince. It's your responsibility to do something about it before it's too late."

"It's not like I have time for magical animals," Marlin sniffed. "I have a kingdom to run."

"You're wrong about the magic, Marlin. I'd give anything to bond with an animal," Emily told him.

"Maybe if you had a real friend like that, you'd believe in magic, too."

"I don't need friends and I don't bond with animals. Besides"—he pointed to her empty wrist—"what good did it do you?"

"I have wonderful friends," she said adamantly.

"If your friends are so great, where are they now when you need them?"

"Baloobah!" A loud crashing noise came from the bushes.

Emily and Marlin bounded to their feet.

"What was that?" The prince's eyes darted across the beach.

Something fuzzy, pink, and purple shuffled from the trees.

"Hey, it's—" Marlin stepped forward.

"Shhh!" Emily held Marlin back. "You'll scare him."

The creature wobbled to the edge of the campfire. A huge grin split his face as he spotted the palm leaves filled with steaming food. Suddenly his body quivered and twisted before snapping back in place.

"grAk!" A huge hiccup sent a burst of blue green twinkles flying through the air.

"That jewel doesn't belong to you," Emily said calmly.

"Blah!"

"The ferret ate your jewel?" Marlin asked.

"He's not a ferret."

"Of course it is." Marlin leaned forward. "Hey, little fella. How'd you get here?"

The purple creature sprang into the merboy's arms, grinning.

"What the—!" Marlin pried the animal from his neck. "Get him off me!"

The creature fell to the sand and grabbed four leaves, shoving them in his mouth. Bits of fruit dribbled down his face, sticking to his fur.

"What's wrong with your ferret?" Marlin asked.

"It's not Ozzie." Emily looked at the merboy. "It's some kind of shapeshifter."

"BWRAAAP!" The creature's mouth opened into a gigantic maw and gave the biggest, loudest burp she'd ever heard.

"That's disgusting." Marlin waved a hand in front of his face.

"Phhbblt!" Sticking his tongue out, the creature started running toward the tree line.

"Don't let him get away!" Emily dove after the little beast, tackling him in the sand.

That purple foot! Wait a minute—"I'd recognize that toe anywhere."

The creature wriggled away and stared at her with big indigo eyes.

"You're not Ozzie, so who are you?"

The purple creature twinkled and spun in a blurry tornado. When it came to a stop, a pink and purple owl blinked blue eyes at Emily.

"Hoooop."

"No, you're not Ariel."

With a twist, the creature spun around, morphing into a purple cat with pink spots.

"Yayayaya."

He was using her jewel to find animals she had connected with.

"Stop it, you're not Lyra, either." This game was starting to upset Emily. "I know who you are—now turn back this instant!"

With a sigh, the creature plopped on his rump and transformed into the purple sea dragon.

"You!" Marlin yelled.

"Pffffft."

"Okay, that's better," the healer said. "Now give me back my jewel."

"Nuh-uh." He shook his head.

"What's your name?" Emily asked the creature.

His deep blue eyes widened. "Rrrrrriiba."

"Nice to meet you," Marlin said. "Now get away from us before you attract more magic."

"You're not going anywhere until I get my jewel back." She looked into the creature's deep blue eyes. "Indigo."

"Dingo?" the creature asked, tilting his head curiously.

"Indigo," Emily repeated. "Your name. Like it, Indi?"

"Byeped." The creature jumped up and scampered around the campfire.

"Come back here, you little jewel gobbler!" Emily scrambled to her feet, chasing him in circles.

Marlin grabbed the purple creature, waggling him back and forth.

"Scribideebibidity." Magic exploded like miniature fireworks as the sea dragon suddenly morphed into a ferocious pink bear—and fell face-first on top of Marlin.

"Help!" the merprince shouted, trapped under the beast's giant belly.

"Leave him alone!" Emily yelled at Marlin.

"I told you." The merboy's voice squeaked. "Magic will never get you anywhere."

PoP!

Emily felt magic tingling all around her.

The pink bear sat comfortably on the sand, a satisfied grin on his face.

"Marlin?" Emily looked around. The merboy had disappeared!

"I'm up here!" Marlin's voice came from somewhere above her head.

The merprince was atop a palm tree, clinging to a branch.

"Finally, we agree on something," Emily said, smiling at Indi.

"Hee hee." Indi leaped to his feet, morphing back into the sea dragon.

"Hey! How do I get down from here?"

Crrrack—THUD!

"That stupid shapeshifter portal popped me!" Marlin exclaimed, stomping back onto the beach, rubbing his rear end. "That's how we both got here."

Emily frowned. What kind of creature *was* this? Unicorns and dragonflies were the only creatures she knew of that could create portals—and this definitely wasn't either.

"Wait, Marlin. If that sea dragon can make portals, he could pop us back."

The merprince considered. "Well, okay. But it's still all your fault."

Emily looked at the grinning creature. Casting Marlin a significant glance, she asked, "Can you take us back to Aquatania?"

Indi shrugged.

"He's probably just being lazy and doesn't want to pop us anywhere." Marlin rolled his eyes and crossed his arms.

"Poptart!" Indigo jumped to his feet, facing the prince.

"I bet you can't even *make* a portal!" Marlin scoffed.

"Blablablabla!" Indi waggled his big rubbery tongue at the prince.

POP!

Emily felt a rushing wind press against her ears. Her stomach twisted as if she were plunging down the highest loop of a roller coaster. Blinding lights dwindled to sparkling points as the din of a hundred voices engulfed them.

When the world steadied, Emily and Marlin found themselves squashed among the strangest creatures she had ever seen.

Chapter 5

"**L**adies and beasties, feast your peepers on this extraordinary item!" A small blue imp wearing a silver jumpsuit leaped across the stage dangling a glowing purple sphere from a chain. "The one and only Eye of Graleth, taken right from the demon's keep. Guaranteed to supercharge any magic!"

Emily stumbled forward as large trolls, warty hobgoblins, and black imps pressed close, gleaming eyes locked onto the magical prize.

"This isn't Aquatania!" Marlin cried.

The imp beamed. "This little beauty is priceless—but for you, I'll make an exception. Now, who'll start the bidding?"

Hands, claws, and spiked tails shot up in the air.

Indi had portal popped Emily and Marlin all right—right into the middle of some bizarre all-creature auction! Torches flamed from nearby towers, lighting the packed market square beyond.

"Sold to the handsome wartbeast," the imp yelled from the stage.

"Woohoo!" A hairy, clawed fist pumped the air triumphantly.

"Where are we?" Emily asked as Marlin guided her out of the throng.

"Thieves Bazaar," Marlin said, stopping at the side of the stage. "Indigo popped us right into the center of Port Tuga!"

"Where is he?" Emily looked around for the shapeshifter.

Circling the market, rows of buildings with thatched awnings formed a dark silhouette against the purple sky. Creatures whose faces were hidden by long, colorful robes inspected mysterious wares in booths that lined the teeming square. Glowing spheres bobbed and floated next to stalls filled with strange bottles and gleaming lamps. Exotic foods and dried herbs perfumed the market with a spicy scent.

"We have to get out of here," Emily whispered, nervously eyeing the motley crowd.

"Right." Marlin dusted off his robes. "I'm a prince. I know how to talk to commoners."

"Marlin, wait—"

The merprince brushed past her and marched onto the stage.

"Ahem!" Marlin struck a regal pose with his shoulders thrown back and his nose in the air. "Good people of Port Tuga." His robes blazed in the lights. "And the rest of you."

Curious creatures swarmed from the shadows.

Armor, sharp teeth, and narrowed eyes glinted in the gloom.

"I am Merprince Marlin III," he announced in a ringing voice. "I'm looking for someone worthy of transporting myself and this great mage." He gestured to Emily.

The crowd buzzed with interest.

"Mage?"

"Merprince?"

"III?"

"Marlin!" Emily hissed.

"Four thousand stars!" someone yelled out.

"I beg your pardon." Marlin blinked.

"Shu bada du mama!"

A spinning whirlwind of pink and purple twirled across the stage. In a flash, it transformed into a pink wartbeast with big red bows in its tusks. Dancing back and forth, it snatched the glowing talisman from the imp.

A troll jumped up and down excitedly. "Five thousand stars!"

"*Eight* thousand for the magic beastie!" An eager dwarf leaped into the air.

"I love you!" a wartbeast called out.

"Do I hear ten thousand?" Marlin called back.

"Marlin!" Emily pulled the merboy out of the spotlight. "What are you doing?"

She gasped as the talisman arced high in the air, falling into Indi's gaping mouth. Lighting up like a sparkler, he transformed again, this time into a big, toothy purple ogre.

"Spit that out!" the blue imp yelled, chasing the ogre in circles.

Ogre Indi cartwheeled across the stage, waggling a giant purple tongue.

The crowd loved the spectacle, yelling and screaming for more.

"Let's take the money and hire a boat," Marlin suggested. "It's that thing's fault we're here."

"I'm not leaving without my jewel," Emily argued.

"Well, there it goes."

"Indi!" Emily shrieked as the ogre took a swan dive off the stage. Streaking into the nearest booth, Indi started gobbling spell vials, potions, gems, and every magical thing in sight.

The crowd surged after him, blanketing the creature in a dark wave.

Emily dashed to the edge of the stage—and was suddenly standing beside Marlin on the opposite side of the bazaar.

"He portal popped us across the market square!" Marlin complained.

"Indi?" Emily whirled around frantically.

The crowded stage area was empty now, except for one enraged blue imp shaking his fist in the air. The shapeshifter was nowhere to be seen.

"I had them in the palm of my fins," Marlin huffed.

"Magic spells!" Hawkers shouted from brightly

colored booths crammed with unusual merchandise. "Fake jewels! Fool your friends!"

Emily gulped. "What are all these creatures doing here?"

"Port Tuga is a hideout for adventurers, magic hunters, and fugitives," Marlin explained. "I bet you can find any magical thing you want here. Probably even another jewel."

"No way." Emily's jewel was totally unique. "Come on, we have to find Indi."

The healer dodged a convoy of covered carts rattling across the cobblestones and scanned the square.

"Knicknoots! Get your knicknoots," came the cry from a nearby booth. "One is never enough!"

"Fascinating." Marlin walked over to inspect a pile of smiling, colorful furballs. Each emitted a pleasant sounding hum. "What do you call this?" he asked the frizzy green-haired dealer.

"It's a knicknoot. Buy four, get eight free."

"Hey, you can't beat that—Emily?"

But Emily barely heard him. Goosebumps prickled up her spine. Someone was watching her. A black-cloaked figure melted into the shadows behind a booth laden with gleaming potions.

Suddenly her view was blocked by a tarnished brass lamp dangling in front of her face.

"Magic lamps!" A wartbeast grinned, sharp white tusks curling from his whiskered snout. "Only been rubbed once."

"Uh, no thanks." Emily stepped back warily.

The cloak of a passing troll caught on the edge of her backpack, revealing a curved dagger cinched to his waist.

"Watch it!" the troll growled.

Marlin grabbed Emily's arm and pulled her away. Snatching two cloaks from a cart, he draped one over himself and handed the other to Emily. "Stop attracting attention."

"I wasn't trying to." Emily slipped the cloak over her head, tucking her red curls under the hood.

"We have to find transport out of here." Marlin looked over several booths.

"Check it out." A bearded gnome with a wide hat displayed racks of brooms, their polished handles gleaming in the lights. "The Nimbot 7000. Fastest flyer I got."

"A broom!" Marlin scoffed. "That's ridiculous. It'll never fly. You got any carpets?"

A glint of light caught Emily's eye. The mysterious cloaked figure lurked in the shadows, watching her.

Emily hunched under her cloak, fear creeping through her body. When she looked back, the figure was gone.

She had to find Indi and get her jewel back. Maybe away from the island's magic shield she could contact her friends.

"Healer."

Emily spun around. Someone had spoken to her

telepathically! She looked up and down winding narrow streets. Shafts of fading sunlight streamed between the buildings, flickering hints of what the darkness hid.

"You are in great danger."

Chills shot up her spine. How could she hear a voice in her mind without her jewel?

She scanned the bazaar, her eyes settling on a squat elf leaning against a booth of stringed instruments. His weathered face was etched with a permanent scowl. Long, pointed ears stuck out at odd angles. A banded knot of hair stood straight atop his flat head.

"Did you say something?" Emily asked the elf.

"Not yet," the elf said, waggling bushy eyebrows.

"Let me handle this," Marlin said, and strode up protectively.

"So, yer looking fer a boot, then." The elf eyed Marlin carefully.

Marlin examined his shoes. "No. Mine are fine."

"I thought I heard yoos be looking for transport."

"Yes, we are," Emily quickly said.

"He said 'boot,'" Marlin said to Emily.

"Aye, you're a smart lad. I be Captain Cribby. I been sailing the briny for many an ear."

"What?"

"We need a fast craft," Emily explained.

"None faster or craftier than the Fearless Flyer."

Marlin ushered the elf into the shadows. "We need to avoid any confrontations."

"You wouldn't be meaning any magical trouble, now would you?"

"What gave you that idea?"

"Take a squinty over there."

Several trolls in leather armor and heavy boots pushed their way through the crowds. One immense troll juggled a handful of singing knicknoots. His buddy slapped them away, pointing in the mage's direction.

Marlin self-consciously pulled his cloak tighter about his royal robes.

"Now, wee wee be goin'?" Cribby whispered.

"What?" Marlin threw his webbed hands in the air.

"We need to get to Aquatania," Emily said.

Cribby whistled. "Ya know, Aquatania is across the freakin' world. Anywhere a mite closer? I hear Boggle Bog is quite nice this time of year."

"No, Aquatania," Marlin snorted contemptuously.

"Can you take us there?" Emily asked.

The elf's beady eyes glittered. "For a fee."

"Once we get there, we'll pay you handsomely," Marlin promised.

"Thank you for the compliment, but I prefer cash."

Emily's hopes sank. "We don't have any money."

Cribby scratched his nose and inspected the prince's sparkly outfit peeking out from under the cloak. "That's a nice robe ya gots there, Princely."

"It's encrusted with pearls and opals."

"That's just crusty enough."

Marlin sighed. "Fine."

"Marlin, are you sure?" Emily asked.

"Yeah, it's okay." Marlin smiled weakly. "I still have my royal rings."

"I'll be needin' those, too, laddie."

"Fine, fine. But not until we're aboard."

"Okay. We're gonna need a scuttlebucket of supplies."

Emily pulled at Marlin's cloak. "We need to find Indi."

Marlin's deep brown eyes studied hers, then flickered to Cribby. "Ten minutes then, at the docks."

"No more, no less, or I be sailin' without ya." Cribby's large red sandals clacked across the cobblestones as he scurried into the crowd.

"Excellent!" Marlin exclaimed. "See, I told you to leave it to me."

"You must leave at once."

Emily's face went ashen. "Who are you?"

"Duh . . . Marlin!" The prince pulled his hood aside quickly.

Instinctively she reached for her wrist—then remembered her jewel was gone. How could she have heard anyone?

This time, Emily closed her eyes and asked with her mind, *"Who are you?"*

"A friend."

Suddenly a roar erupted across the crowded

square. A purple and pink blur flew through the air, bouncing over the crowd.

"Indi!"

Back to his odd sea dragon form, the shapeshifter tore through a striped canvas awning and ricocheted through booths, demolishing rows of shelves. Spell vials, wands, and crystals went flying as the creature stuffed everything he could into his mouth.

"Indi!" Emily bolted across the busy square.

Marlin followed her, then skidded to a stop.

The group of trolls had surrounded Indi. One of the brutes picked him up, shaking him furiously. The troll scratched his head as Indi whirled in rainbow colors.

Marlin casually stepped up. "Excuse me, my good troll."

The troll stared down at the merboy. He was easily three times Marlin's size, with biceps so huge, they looked like hams, and thighs as thick as tree trunks.

"Would you be so kind as to return the purple . . . um . . . dragon."

"Get lost!" The troll shoved Marlin with a huge hand.

Marlin was either incredibly brave, or just stupid.

"Now look here, I am Prince Mar—"

The troll pushed his muzzle in Marlin's face. "We don't like your kind."

"You mean the kind with clean breath?"

A crowd gathered around them, grumbling loudly.

"Hey, it's that merprince!"

"And the mage."

"Indi, pop us out of here!" Emily pleaded with the sea dragon.

Emily and Marlin disappeared in a flash. With a *POP*, they materialized two feet to the left.

Indi belched a rainbow of sparkles. Eyes crossed and tongue lolling, he hung limp in the troll's hands.

"Har har!" The trolls laughed. "Make more magic, mage."

"Leave us alone!" Marlin gallantly stepped in front of Emily. "Don't worry," he whispered to her. "I'm schooled in protecting six different types of princesses."

Emily gulped. "But I'm not a princess."

"Oh. Then run!"

But there was nowhere to go. The trolls pressed in, backing them against a building.

"A mage and a merprince." A silver dagger glinted in the troll leader's massive hand. "Nice."

Emily had to do something—and fast! But what?

"Use your magic."

Magic? But what could she do without her jewel?

"You don't need your jewel." The strange voice echoed in Emily's mind again. *"Control their thoughts— make them think something else."*

Panic rising, Emily reached out. A pulsing strength seemed to grow from the center of her being.

"Now hear their thoughts."

Not knowing what else to do, Emily concentrated, focusing her will like a laser. Shadows played across the stalls, turning and gleaming in slow motion. Lights floated in a dreamlike haze. The bazaar took on a surreal glow as shapes split into double vision.

"Focus."

Random words fluttered across her mind. Emily was only half conscious of the thoughts until she paid attention. Suddenly the background noise of a hundred different conversations flooded her mind.

"Good. Now listen to the words."

The hum of the crowd faded to a soft buzz as distinct voices erupted in her mind.

"Stupid mages! It's their fault I'm stuck here."

"I'll make a fortune with that magic creature."

"I wish I had a knicknoot."

The thoughts flowed through her mind like water.

"With a magic jewel, I can become as powerful as the Dark Sorceress, and rule all of Aldenmor!"

"If that mage doesn't figure out how to get us out of here, I'm not inviting her to Wave Fest II."

The calm, cool voice broke through the throng. *"Tell them they don't want this magic creature."*

Emily felt her magic lock onto their thoughts.

"You don't want this magic creature," she called in her mind.

The trolls' eyes glazed over. Their bodies went limp.

"Drop the sea dragon or I'll . . . really get mad!" Marlin threatened, doing his best to look fierce.

"I don't want this magic thing," the large troll mumbled in a daze, letting Indi slip to the ground.

"Now, that's much better," Marlin said, puffing out his chest.

Emily scooped up the sea dragon.

"Beebee!"

"Shhh!"

"beeebeee."

"Tell them you were never here, you never existed."

Emily sent the telepathic message to the trolls. *"We were never here, you never saw us, we never existed."*

"They were never here. We never saw them. They never existed."

"Who?" a blue troll asked.

"I dunno. I'm hungry, let's go to Bob's Big Buoy."

The creatures shuffled back, bumping into one another as they wandered into the crowded square.

Emily let out her breath, amazed. She could always sense what other people were feeling, but had no idea she could actually change what they were thinking. It was like she had erased their thoughts and replaced them with her own.

"What did you do?" Marlin asked, shocked. The crowd just milled around, paying no attention to them.

Emily inhaled sharply. "Whatever I did, I don't know how long it will last."

She scanned the mysterious alleyways and winding streets. "Which way to the docks?"

"This way, mage," the voice guided her forward.

This was totally creepy. But whoever it was had just saved them.

"Come on." Marlin guided her down a corridor off the bazaar.

"No. This way." Emily hurried down an alley in the opposite direction, holding Indi close inside her cloak. Marlin had little choice but to follow her lead.

Indi dangled in her arms, leaving a trail of twinkly bits with each burp.

"You ate too much junk," Emily scolded.

"Blahhhhp."

"He has Indi-gestion," the merprince cracked.

Emily's head swam as she felt her healing magic mixed together with every magical thing Indi had swallowed. At least she still had a connection to her jewel, however faint.

"I can see the docks!" Marlin exclaimed.

The smell of salt water wafted in the wind as they raced out of the alleyway. The streets all ran downhill, converging onto a long boardwalk above the port. Several ramps angled down to rows of rickety wooden docks below the seawall. Boats of every size and shape were preparing to moor for the night.

Emily gasped and skidded to a stop, forcing Marlin to barrel into her.

Two large, nasty-looking, lizard-like creatures with sharp, gleaming teeth blocked the way. Emily recognized them. So did the merprince.

"Bulwoggles!" Marlin cried.

"I smell magic." A bulwoggle smacked his lips, revealing pointed fangs.

"Well, well, the merprince and the mage," the other growled, yellow lizard eyes staring hungrily at the glowing dragon. "You're not thinking of leaving, are you?"

"Emily, do your mind trick again," Marlin urged.

The healer tried to pierce the creatures' minds like she'd done before. But this time it didn't work. A weird sensation tickled along Emily's spine as bright sparkles exploded in her head. For a second, she lost her breath.

The bulwoggles suddenly froze stone still, lizard eyes opened in surprise.

"It gets easier," a cool voice spoke. "You don't have the skill yet."

That voice! Emily whirled around.

A tall woman shrouded in a black cloak stepped from the alley.

"It was you, wasn't it?" Emily's eyes opened wide.

"Who the heck are you?" Marlin demanded.

The woman threw back her hood, revealing a startlingly beautiful face. "I am a wizard."

Chapter 6

"**M**ove to the docks," the woman commanded. "Now."

Who *was* this person? Emily clutched Indi tightly. She could feel her jewel thrumming inside the sea dragon.

"Come on, Emily." Marlin helped her down the ramp and onto the gently swaying docks. Beyond, the blues and blacks of the ocean stretched to the infinite horizon. Funny, Emily thought. There was no sign of the island she and Marlin had been stranded on.

"Where's Cribby?" Marlin asked, scanning sailing craft of all sizes and shapes.

But Emily was more concerned about the sudden appearance of the stranger. She watched the woman slowly back down the ramp, the bulwoggles still locked in her spell.

"How do you know me?" Emily asked.

"My name is Miranda. I helped you escape; that's enough for now." Her tone was cool as ice. "Trust me."

Emily tried to keep her breath steady. Something didn't feel right.

"Here I be!" Cribby's voice suddenly called out.

"Over there," Marlin said, and pointed.

A large, three-masted schooner was pulling majestically up to the docks.

They broke into a run.

But the magnificent vessel glided past, revealing a much smaller craft.

Marlin screeched to a stop, mouth open in shock. Cribby whistled happily, bailing sea water out of a beat-up old scow, its single mast bent under weather-beaten sails.

"This is your boat?!" Marlin cried.

"Aye, she is," the sea elf said, proudly puffing out his chest. "A real piece o' work." He tossed a rope to the shocked merprince.

Planks of mismatched wood haphazardly nailed together formed a small cabin behind the mast. A shallow cockpit in the helm was crammed with barrels, rope, a small anchor, and assorted supplies.

"I am not getting on this," Marlin declared.

"There they are!" a group of voices echoed over the waters.

Dozens of creatures stormed onto the docks, weapons gleaming in the fading sun.

"They're trying to get away!" someone yelled.

"Come back with our magic!" another commanded.

The bulwoggles snapped out of their trance, roaring along with the crowd.

"What happened to the spells?" Emily cried.

The woman shrugged. "We're a little low on magic. They wore off."

The planks shifted as the angry mob thundered down the ramps. Battle-axes, swords, pitchforks, and blazing balls of magic fired into the evening skies.

"Clam almighty!" Cribby tossed his buckets and leaped to the steering wheel.

A flash of red crackled from Miranda's long fingers. Several barrels suddenly tumbled down the docks, bowling into the crowd.

One of the bulwoggles deftly launched himself over the barrels, sword drawn, yellow eyes flashing anger.

Miranda swung her arm, creating a sparkling shield.

Grinning, the bulwoggle reached behind his back and withdrew a long, wicked-looking sword. He swiped it through the air a few times, testing its weight. With a bloodcurdling cry, the monster smashed it into the shield, sending splinters of light flying.

"Hurry up!" Miranda yelled.

"Come back here, Cribby!" Marlin grabbed the rope attached to the craft. His heels slid across the wooden planks as he tried to hold on.

"Ye better heave ho, or I go!" the sea elf called out.

With one last doubtful look at the boat, Marlin heaved himself aboard, pulling Emily after him.

"Merman the mainsail!" Cribby called out, pulling the rigging taut as the boat rocked dangerously.

Marlin tripped over the ropes as the flimsy sail unfurled from the mast.

We don't have enough time, Emily thought as she watched Miranda back toward the boat. Wizard or no wizard, the woman couldn't hold off the bulwoggles for long, let alone the entire crowd. They'd never make it!

Panic suddenly gripped Emily. Where was Indi? In the confusion, she had lost him!

"HiC!"

The little sea dragon sat on the dock, burping a flurry of magic.

The bulwoggles stopped, confused by the strange creature.

With another hiccup, Indi expanded, growing twice as big as the bulwoggles.

"What in the—Indi?" Emily gasped.

Body rippling, a green scorpion tail emerged from one end of Indi's torso, a snarling lion's head taking shape from the other.

"Chimera!" someone yelled.

With a roar, chimera Indi's spiked tail ripped through the wooden boards.

The bulwoggles leaped out of the way of the fearsome half lion, half scorpion.

With a ferocious snarl, chimera Indi hiccupped and shrank into a—pink bunny.

"It's just a bunny rabbit!"

Laughter erupted as the crowd surged closer.

The bunny twitched its whiskers—"hic!"—and expanded. Sharp, pointy teeth sprang from an elongated mouth. Red eyes opened from a wolf-like head, and purple hair sprang from Indi's body.

"Werebeast!"

"A Har!" Werebeast Indi stomped up the docks, forcing the crowd back, giving Cribby time to set sail.

With one last enormous belch, Indi toppled over a pile of crates. Then, like a balloon losing air, the creature faded from view.

"Anchors away!" Cribby firmly spun the wheel as the boat pulled out of the harbor.

Back to his sea dragon form, Indi staggered to the end of the dock, gazing at Emily with wide eyes. Pieces of him sparkled as he tried to use Emily's magic to shapeshift.

"Wait!" Emily ran to the stern, causing the Flyer to tilt alarmingly.

"Let him turn into a whale and swim to us," Marlin said.

"He can't," Emily cried. "He used all his magic to save us."

"Emeemee." The creature held out his stubby arms.

The bulwoggles reached for the shapeshifter. But before they could grab him, Indi fell forward, tumbling into the water.

Cribby held the wheel firmly as the Flyer headed for the breakwater. "Off we go, then."

"Indi!" Emily screamed, searching the churning waters. There was no sign of him. Spray and foam obscured Emily's view as she scrambled over the railing.

"No, wait!" Marlin pulled the struggling girl back. "I'm a merboy." His mouth twitched with a quick smile. "I can hold my breath for twenty minutes . . . I think."

Before she could protest, Marlin threw off his robe and dove into the dark waters.

"Turn us around!" Emily commanded Cribby.

"Are ye all mad?" The sea elf held the sail taut with one hand, gripping the wheel with the other. "We'll never make it outta here!"

Water sloshed over the prow as the Flyer smacked into turbulent crests of surging waves.

Emily hung on to the railing, watching for any signs of the merboy.

"He'll never catch up!" she fretted.

But suddenly a pink and purple ball bobbed to the surface, held aloft by a pair of light green arms. Marlin was moving through the water at amazing speed. In no time the pair was alongside the boat.

Emily stared openmouthed. "How did you swim so fast?"

"I didn't." Marlin was swiftly raised above the surface, astride an amazing creature. Huge sea green eyes blinked from a wide, horse-like head. Purple and green sparkles ran down her scales.

A wild sea dragon!

"Help!" Marlin clutched the creature's neck.

"Give me your hand." Emily reached out.

The dragon's head swung to the boat and locked eyes with Emily. Instantly, she felt the creature's pain. The dragon was suffering the same virus as the sea dragons in Aquatania.

"Save the merboy," the dragon's voice cried in Emily's mind.

Miranda helped Emily hoist the boy on board. In an instant, he was sprawled onto the deck, out of breath. Indi landed with a loud *THUMP!*

"Avast, ye crabbers!" Cribby yelled, turning the boat abruptly. "I'm coming aboot!"

"What?" Emily asked.

With a rush, the boom swung dangerously across the deck, missing Emily's head by inches. Sails filled out as the vessel leaned into the wind and sped off.

With a last look, the incredible sea dragon dove into the water, glistening fins vanishing in a spray of foam.

"Emily, you see that?" The excited boy pointed.

"That was totally amazing!"

"Finally, we're all on board." Cribby smiled, heading the Fearless Flyer into open waters. "Swift as a gull, she is. Off wee bee—"

"Niva!" Marlin yelled.

"Turn around!" Cribby shouted. "Wait—who's Niva?"

"The sea dragon." Marlin dashed over to the stern, searching the waves.

"I ain't taking a sea dragon on board, ya barnacle brain!" the elf captain cried.

Emily's eyes widened. "You heard her?"

Marlin stumbled, his face reflecting fear and wonder. "How . . . why?"

"Easy." Emily eased him back to the cabin, feeling his forehead and checking his pulse.

"I'm okay," Marlin said, smiling weakly. "We made it."

"Of course we made it!" Cribby boasted as the sails snapped in the wind. "I ain't Cribby the sea elf for nothing."

"Good job, elf," Miranda said.

"Hooya!" Cribby slapped a hand on her back. "Hey—who are you?"

Emily crouched by Indi. The shapeshifter had coiled into a tight ball. She could barely sense her jewel, pulsing softly inside, keeping him alive.

"What's wrong with him?" Marlin asked.

"He's run out of magic," Emily said worriedly, then turned to Miranda. "You're a wizard. Can you help him?"

"I believe I can," the tall woman said, and mysteriously smiled.

"What's a wizard?" Marlin asked.

"A magic master. There will be time for answers later." The woman's hypnotic voice washed over Emily. "You must all rest now."

The salty sea air made knots of Emily's curls. She gazed at the golden sun sinking into the ocean. Little by little, she felt free, as if she hadn't a worry in the world. At last she was on her way to Aquatania. Her heart soared, knowing she would soon be with Ozzie, Kara, Adriane, and her other friends. Everything was going to be all right.

But first she needed to rest for a few minutes. Cribby and Marlin were nodding off, sinking to the deck.

She was so tired . . . so tired.

The last rays of sunset vanished as darkness closed in.

Chapter 7

"**A**re you sure it's here?" Lorren asked.

The sky had darkened to glowing purple as the group huddled around Tasha. Mount Hope loomed above them, its majestic peak towering over mountains that stretched hundreds of miles on either side.

"See those trees?" Zach pointed to a section of thick forest behind them. A line of firs stood in a tight formation, as if pointing to a wooded hollow. "Many hidden portals are identified by natural markers. I bet that's one of them."

"It's right here on the fairy map," the goblin girl confirmed, then turned to Adriane and Kara. "How are you at opening portals?"

"My unicorn magic can open them," said Kara.

"Okay. We'll use the signals from Emily's jewel to guide us through." Tasha pushed a series of buttons. "Ozzie will lock on to the rainbow stone . . . which is right—"

"Right where?" The ferret stuck his snout close to the screen.

Tasha's green forehead wrinkled in concentration.

"What's wrong?" Adriane asked.

"These readings—" Tasha pointed to the colors streaming onto her jewel locator—"it's definitely Emily's jewel."

"But?" Ozzie prompted her.

"Something's wrong. See there—these purples are darker."

"What does that mean?" Kara asked.

Tasha took a deep breath, then her words came rushing out: "Emily's magic is very weak. It's almost gone."

The dull roar of wind rushing down the mountain seemed supernaturally loud.

"Then what are we waiting for!" Ozzie shouted.

The group hopped onto bats, cat, and dragon.

"Let's do it." Kara raised her unicorn jewel, crisscrossing the air with diamond pink sparkles.

The magic of the blazing star turned bright red, swirling into a deep circle of lights. In a surge of energy, an immense portal flashed open. Inside, lightning spiked along looping strands of stars.

Adriane, Zach, and Ozzie raised their jewels.

"Everybody twist beams of magic together into a rope," Tasha instructed, locking the locations of the other three portals into her magic meter. "We'll need the strongest force possible to pull us through all four portals."

Silver light blazed from Adriane's wrist as she coiled an arc of wolf magic overhead.

"I'll take the lead. I know how to braid." Kara wove a band of blazing pink power around the wolf magic. The two crackling beams bounced apart, once again repelled by each other.

"Zach," Tasha cried. "Can you hold them together?"

The boy shot a beam of red dragon magic, binding the pink and silver strands together. The rope crackled but held firm.

"Okay, then." Kara twisted the beams into a shimmering braid. With a tug, she pulled tight.

The warrior belted one end of the magic braid around the group, holding them together.

"We go on one." Adriane swung the other end over her head.

"Ready . . ." Kara called out.

Faster and faster, the chain swung like a lasso, gathering power.

"Set . . ." Zach leaned forward in Drake's saddle.

Lights flared from the portal, attracted to the mages' brilliant magic.

"One!" Ozzie screamed.

The warrior flung the glowing chain through the portal.

"Hold it steady!" Tasha called out.

The rope uncoiled at alarming speed, shooting through the open gateway.

"We're through the second one," Tasha announced,

following the chain's path as it stretched across the small screen. "We need more power!"

Drake roared, sending a blast of dragon fire blazing through Zach's jewel.

"We're through the third!" Tasha cried. "Ozzie, go!"

Ozzie squeezed his eyes shut in concentration as ferret magic streamed from his gem. Power surged along the rope as he reached for Emily's jewel. With a shuddering jolt, ferret fur stood on end. "I got her!"

"Hang on!" Adriane yelled.

The rope snapped taut, yanking everyone into the swirling abyss.

❧ ❧ ❧

Wind ruffled Emily's copper curls as the Fearless Flyer coasted across endless ocean.

Something tickled at the back of her mind. Thoughts were cloudy, unfocused, just out of reach. She couldn't remember exactly what had happened after they'd escaped Port Tuga. They'd learned little from the strange woman, Miranda. She was a wizard, a magic master, yet carried no jewel. She had escaped with them from Port Tuga—then everyone suddenly fell asleep.

The dark shape of Cribby slouched against the wheel, gently snoring. Marlin dozed by the mast. Indi lay curled in a tight ball, motionless and barely breathing.

"Healer."

Emily slowly turned.

Miranda stood tall and regal at the prow. Brilliant swathes of crystal starlight reflected from the ocean's surface, as if she were enveloped in the magic web itself.

"Tell me." Miranda's voice drew Emily closer. "Why are you so troubled?"

"I . . . lost my healing jewel, and the sea dragons are sick."

"Ah." Miranda nodded. "You can't heal them."

Emily shook her head.

Miranda leaned forward, earnest and sincere. "I can help you."

Emily wanted to believe. She had worked just as hard as Kara and Adriane, but no matter what she did, she seemed to get nowhere, or just make things worse.

"But how could I use magic without my jewel?" Emily twisted her empty silver bracelet. "I don't even have a bonded animal."

"I've never needed a jewel or an animal." The woman's eyes flared. "You don't, either—you never have."

Emily caught her breath.

"Jewels and bonded animals enhance magic. But you risk much if you rely solely on them." The voice wormed its way into Emily. "You never know who will fail you. Believe me, the magic is stronger alone."

No. Emily shook her head. Miranda's words went

against everything Emily believed. Bonding with animals always made the strongest magic.

And yet, she remembered, she had spoken to Lyra *before* she had found her rainbow stone. And Kara had used magic for months before finding *her* unicorn jewel.

Miranda echoed her thoughts. "You can learn to control magic freely—dependent on no one."

Silvery light illuminated Miranda's pale face. For a heartbeat, Emily thought she saw the woman's sharp features shimmer and blur before snapping back into focus.

"Who are you?"

"I was a mage . . . once. My friends and I were on a quest much like yours. To find Avalon."

Emily, caught in the spell of the hypnotic voice, waited for her to continue.

"I'm afraid our story doesn't have a happy ending. We never found the home of magic."

"We released magic from Avalon," Emily said proudly. "That's how we helped heal Aldenmor."

Miranda's hard gaze held Emily under her spell. "Yes, you found magic—but it did not come from Avalon."

"How do you know that?"

Miranda smiled bitterly. "Because the magic you found belonged to me."

"What?" the healer exclaimed. "But the Fairimentals chose us to find Avalon."

"The Fairimentals *used* you to steal my magic."

This made no sense. If Miranda was right about jewels, animals, and Avalon, then everything Emily knew about magic was a lie.

"Then where did *your* magic come from?" Emily asked.

"That, my dear, is what your special talent is all about." Miranda's eyes locked on hers. "You have used magic to heal wounds. But you can do so much more."

"Like I did with those creatures in the bazaar." Emily shuddered. Using her magic to manipulate the thoughts and emotions of others had worked, but felt all wrong.

"That is only the beginning. Perhaps what ails the sea dragons is not physical."

Suddenly Emily realized why she couldn't help the sea dragons. It was their *magic* that needed healing. But how was she supposed to heal something she couldn't see?

The first rays of dawn cast a twinkling pink haze over the boat.

In the dim shadows, the woman smiled dangerously. "You are a healer. You can learn to see the magic itself, shape it however you desire."

If she didn't do something, the last of the sea dragons were going to die. A true healer would risk anything to save those animals.

Emily faced the woman. "Show me."

Miranda shifted her gaze to the still form of Indi. "Start with what you know."

"I can't. He ate my jewel," Emily reminded her.

"You should be glad. You're free now."

Concentrating, Emily stared at Indi. But all she saw was a purple and pink ball. Her hazel eyes stung with frustrated tears.

"Look harder."

Emily felt Miranda's voice in her mind, guiding her like she'd done back at the bazaar. The healer looked through the pink scales and purple toes—sensing something beyond Indi's physical appearance—something she'd always felt, but had never been able to see before.

Suddenly Indi began to pulse with rainbow lights, as if a switch had been turned on. The blues and greens of her healing gem seemed to come from inside out, swirling around him in a glittering halo. It mixed with Indi's own pink and purple magic.

"I see it," she breathed.

"Every creature has a magic aura." Miranda gently turned the girl toward the ocean. *"Now look."*

In a heartbeat, Emily felt the vastness of the ocean surround her. Brilliant flares gleamed beneath the surface, blinking to the horizon and beyond.

Miranda smiled, eyes ablaze, drawing the healer alongside her. *"Open yourself to their magic."*

Exquisite auras danced around her like threads of woven starlight. She was seeing the magic of all the animals in the ocean!

"Weave a web so your magic can reach all the animals."

Strands of light shone from each animal's aura blurring into a kaleidoscope of shifting magic, dissolving, re-forming. Reaching out in her mind, Emily grasped the strands, weaving them together into a new pattern—a web.

"That's it. Now find the strongest magic."

Was it really so easy, as Miranda said, to take that magic and use it however she desired?

The healer reached deeper, following the strands to the web's center. Brilliant magic swirled in blues, greens, and silver, dazzling her senses. Hundreds of objects gleamed in a place of liquid light—jewels! The stones pulsed and sparkled with magic beyond her wildest dreams!

"See how they come to you."

Raw magical energy surged along the web, drawn to the healer's touch. Suddenly, the bright lights morphed to a deep red, seeping like blood as the frightening realization hit. It wasn't just Meerka and the other sea dragons that were sick. It was every creature in the ocean.

"Healer!"

One voice sounded in her mind, then another, and another, growing into a deafening chorus.

"Help us!"

The rush of magic was overwhelming. Emily was so deeply connected, she couldn't distinguish between her own feelings and those of the thousands of animals caught in her web of magic. There were so many lost and hurt, desperate for help. How could she heal them all?

"Help us, healer!"

Still, they came to her, giving their magic freely, trusting Emily, the healer.

"What should I do?" Emily cried out.

"You've already done it."

The woman's smile curled into a vicious sneer.

Pain struck like a sledgehammer as Miranda wrenched the magic from Emily.

Panicked screams exploded in her head.

"What are you doing to them?"

And then, the worst of it hit her: It was Emily, without even realizing it, taking the magic of all these innocent creatures, strangling their very life-force. And Miranda, in turn, was taking it from her. Using her.

Like wildfire, the power grew as more and more animals became caught in the web of Emily's awesome power.

"It's time you learned the truth."

The woman stood in front of her, arms spread wide as glowing strands swirled around her, rising into an inferno of power as she fed on the magic Emily had gathered.

"Great magic comes through pain. This is your magic, healer!"

Emily struggled to focus, but she was losing, drowning in the agony of the animals.

"Help me!" the girl tried to scream.

But there was no Emily.

Only the nightmare of a girl out of control, using the full force of her magic to destroy all that she loved most.

Chapter 8

Trees, mountains, and lakes sped by in a blur of color as Drake, Nightwing, Gertie, and Lyra tumbled from the portal. The chain of magic streaked across the sky like a floating river of light, pulling them forward at blinding speed.

"Something is attacking my magic!" Dreamer howled.

"Dreamer!" Adriane tore her magic away from the rope to help her packmate.

Drake roared as the chain buckled, erupting in a flurry of sparks.

Tasha clung to Gertie as the bat screeched in agony. "We're only through the third portal!"

In the distance, the fourth portal swirled into sight.

Ozzie hung on frantically as Lyra spiraled out of control, sharp pain searing through her.

Kara wrenched her magic from the rope and gave it to her bonded.

"Keep that rope together!" Zach yelled, trying to hold Drake steady.

"What's wrong with the animals?" Lorren shouted over Nightwing's screeches.

"What did you do?" Kara yelled at Adriane.

"Me? What did *you* do?" the warrior demanded.

"Their magic is being ripped apart!" Tasha clung to Gertie's saddle with one hand, tweaking her magic meter with the other. "It's coming from Emily!"

The group soared across the sky, trailing magic like a comet.

"I thought you said her magic was weak," Adriane called to Tasha.

"Something's happened!" Tasha shouted back. "It's been supercharged!"

"Agagagagagag," Ozzie's clenched teeth chattered as he tried to filter the thunderous power of Emily's magic. "She needs our help!"

"Our only shot is to reach Emily through her jewel!" Tasha shouted.

"I've still got her!" Ozzie called, arms wrapped tight around Lyra's neck.

"Channel your magic through the ferret stone," Tasha instructed.

"I've got it!" Fiery unicorn power streamed from Kara's jewel.

"Back off!" Silvery magic sprang from Adriane's gem.

"I know what I'm doing." Kara's jewel flared with pink and red sparks as she struggled against the wolf magic.

"So do I." Adriane's jewel radiated rings of silver.

Glowing beams of unicorn and wolf magic zapped into Ozzie's gem.

"gAh!"

The ferret stone blazed as wolf and unicorn power collided with explosive force. Magic sizzled over the rope, ripping it to shreds.

Roaring in pain, Drake plummeted to the ground.

Tasha and Gertie tumbled head over ear.

Nightwing fell from the sky, Lorren and Kara hanging on.

Propelled by the blast of magic, Ozzie and Lyra careened into the fourth portal.

"Ahhhh!"

❧   ❧   ❧

The agonized scream tore through Emily as she burst into the operating room. The Stonehill Animal Hospital tilted at odd angles as the large creature thrashed on the table.

In shaky slow motion, a terrifying image came into focus. Lyra lay before her, the cat's beautiful orange fur ravaged with deep burns.

"No!" Emily recoiled from the horrible sight.

That had been the first contact Emily had ever made with a magical animal—a discovery that should have been wondrous and joyful.

As if in a dream, Emily saw herself freeze, unable to help the injured cat.

I'm sorry, she wanted to scream. Lyra's mangled body shimmered as the hospital melted into dizzying light

flash

the night sky blazed with magic. Lights illuminated the trees surrounding the portal field in Ravenswood. Heart pounding, clothes damp with sweat, Emily leaned over the purple bearlike creature lying on the grass. His weakened body was translucent, ripped apart by glowing Black Fire.

"Phel." Emily could hardly breathe. The fairy creature had taught her about healing. Now he needed her. Desperately she tried to summon her magic—but it wouldn't come. She couldn't heal him. Her worst nightmares had come to life, a chilling reminder of her helplessness and failure

flash

bright sun cut through the trees, tilting the world upside down. Gasping for breath, Emily hit the bottom of the muddy incline. An injured owl lay in the ditch: Ariel! The snow owl's exquisite feathers were burned beyond recognition.

Emily knew she should do something. But in her secret heart of hearts, she wanted to run away.

Was she reliving these awful memories, or was something happening to her now? It didn't matter. Touching the core of her magic was like exposing a raw nerve. It was agonizing, unbearable pain

flash

a white unicorn appeared, her magnificent horn severed. Confusion, shame, and fear hit Emily like she was seeing Lorelei for the first time. The beautiful unicorn had been injured, alone, without her magic, without her friends.

Yet sensing Emily's need, the unicorn gifted her with a sweet melody, a healing song of friendship and love—the song she and Emily had made their own.

Frantic, Emily reached for the unicorn, allowing the bond to envelop her. The magic steadied, and she focused on the thousands of animals still trapped in her web.

Suddenly, soothing cool greens and blues swept over her. It felt familiar and calming. It was her rainbow stone.

The screams of the animals fell away one by one—freed from her twisted web of magic. The song of Lorelei rang out, and it filled Emily with the truth.

Emily *had* healed Lorelei, just as she had healed

the others. They were healthy and whole. But their pain was forever lodged in her heart, a dark fear that uncoiled each time she had to use her power. It was her burden, her job to keep everyone strong. But who was supposed to heal her?

"*Em-il-ee,*" a voice beckoned.

"Indi?"

The sea dragon sat before her. Wide blue eyes seemed to fill with understanding. For the first time, she felt something solid and real coming from the shapeshifter. Indi was tapping into her rainbow stone. Was he trying to help find an animal that would balance her? Bond with her? Dream-like, the creature that was Indi grew taller, shimmering, until the most beautiful unicorn she had ever seen was standing in front of her.

His silky coat shone purple and pink, swirling like sunset skies. His horn blazed like a brilliant rainbow, a shining beacon guiding her from the dark places of her heart. It was magic only a true bonded animal could give.

"*Emilee . . .*"

"Emily! Wake up!"

The healer came to herself with a start. Her head ached from the terrible strain of using so much magic. "Indi?"

"No, it's me, Marlin!" His voice sounded far away, but when she turned her head, he was standing right there. "Hurry, you have to see this!"

"What happened?" Why did she feel so drained, like she'd just run a marathon?

"You were in some kind of trance." Marlin brushed Emily's hair out of her face, looking deep into her eyes.

"Trance . . ." Emily scrambled to her feet. "Where's Miranda?"

"Who?"

"The woman who came on board with us!"

Marlin frowned. "What are you talking about? There was no one else with us."

Had it all been a dream? It'd seemed so real. All those animals crying out because her magic *hurt* them, and then Indi, her bonded, saving her, returning her to reality. Emily hugged herself, suddenly cold.

"I don't know how you did it, but you healed it, him, whatever." Marlin pointed across the deck.

An amazing purple and pink unicorn colt pranced happily about the deck. His horn sparkled with rainbow magic—her healing jewel!

"Indi?"

"Look at me!" Indi the unicorn exclaimed, kicking up his glittering hooves.

Emily stared in wonder at the transformed shapeshifter. Instantly she felt the strong connection, unlike anything she had experienced before. It was as if a part of her danced within the creature. It had finally happened—she had bonded with a magical animal!

"Clamdoodle!" Cribby sputtered, frantically spinning the ship's wheel. "Ya better get yer barnacles over here!"

Indi trotted across the deck, his horn swirling blues and greens.

Emily gazed out over the ocean, appalled.

The water was littered with bodies.

"The sea beasties are belly up!" Cribby pointed to the limply floating creatures.

Fear clamped around Emily's heart like a vise.

"Are they all dead?" Marlin asked in horror.

She tentatively reached out, sweeping her magic over the waters. Red auras bloomed like a sea of blood. Their sickness was much worse. Had she done this?

"They're not dead," Emily declared. "But they're so weak."

Indi leaned his head over her shoulder, concerned and protective.

"Holy mackerel!" Cribby yelled.

"Where?" Marlin scanned the ocean.

"Over there!"

Black fins sliced through the water. Thrashing tails propelled sleek beasts toward the helpless animals.

"Sea wolves!" Marlin exclaimed.

A huge sharklike creature lunged to the surface, jaws closing around a squirming dolphin.

"They're preying on the weak animals." Emily felt sick to her stomach.

In a whirl of motion, several wolves were suddenly

knocked backward by a large green and purple creature.

"Oh, no!" Marlin exclaimed.

Niva burst through the water, leaping into the air. She roared loudly, shaking the sails and rattling the rigging.

"Your sea dragon!" Emily exclaimed, her eyes wide with shock.

Wolf heads, slick with matted fur, broke to the surface. The sea wolf pack headed straight toward Niva!

"She must have followed us from Port Tuga! Emily, do something!" Marlin implored. "She's too weak to get away!"

Emily swung her wrist up automatically, forgetting for a second that her jewel was gone. Bright patterns of magic shifted before her eyes. Momentarily, she panicked. What if her magic only made it worse?

"I . . . can't." She wrenched her power back from the chaos.

The wolves tightened their circle, snapping razor teeth as the weak sea dragon bravely tried to defend herself.

The glint of a knife caught Emily's eye. Marlin was climbing out on the railing.

"Marlin!" Emily screamed.

"Niva!" Marlin dove into the water between his sea dragon and the snarling sea wolves. Emily looked on in horror as the merprince disappeared amid black fins and gleaming teeth.

Chapter 9

"**M**arlin!" Emily screamed, frantically searching the thrashing waters. Magic surged inside her, struggling to break free. She shoved it aside, terrified of its power.

And then the merboy's head surfaced amid the pack, followed by his dagger, slashing furiously.

"Stay away from my sea dragon!" Marlin smacked a sea wolf on its wide gray snout.

"Ack, they're gonna eat the merboy!" Cribby hopped from foot to foot.

Emily watched helplessly as the sharks bore down on Marlin and Niva. There was no way the merboy could fight off so many. She had to do something.

"*I help.*" Indi's wide eyes caught Emily's gaze.

Instantly, the magic of her healing jewel soothed her, focusing her thoughts. Maybe she could use her magic after all—with Indi.

"Okay. Keep the sea wolves away from Marlin," she instructed, concentrating on the pulsing center of their magic, hers and Indi's.

The unicorn nodded, guiding their magic over the

water in a bright wave. Emily's breath caught as a fierce bolt suddenly blazed from Indi's horn. Water exploded as magic tore across the ocean like a rocket out of control.

"Stop!" With all of her will, she wrenched the magic back.

Amid the frightened animals, several sea wolves floated, their lifeless bodies twisted in unnatural angles.

"No," Emily breathed. She had only meant to repel the sea wolves, not kill them. She turned to the unicorn, horrified. "What did you do?"

Indi shrank back, head lowered in shame.

"Come on, lad." Cribby gave Marlin a hand as he scrambled back onto the boat.

"Thanks." The merprince slicked his wet hair back. "Emily, are you okay?"

Emily's eyes were locked on the dead sea wolves, tears running down her cheeks. All she had ever wanted was to use magic with a bonded animal. Now look what she had done. "He . . . I killed them."

"Emily," Marlin said softly.

"I-I just wanted the sea wolves to go away," she stammered. Her whole body shook. What if her magic had killed the entire pack? Or the other animals? They were only acting on instinct, like they were supposed to.

"There was nothing else you could have done. Besides, the sea wolves would have eaten Niva."

"Leave me alone." She walked to the stern and slumped against the railing, head in her hands.

The rising sun gilded the water, covering the world in warm gold.

Shyly, Indi approached her from the shadows. The creature's bright aura faded as he sensed her disappointment.

"*I do bad?*"

Emily looked into his deep indigo eyes, and her anger fell away. Somehow he had used her magic and transformed himself into a unicorn, an animal she loved deeply. He had drawn her out of her trance and its dark visions, had brought her back to herself. But he wasn't really a unicorn. He was just in the shape of a unicorn. He had no time to learn to grow. How was he supposed to know how to use their magic? Kara and Adriane had spent months working with their bonded animals, learning together.

"I didn't know your magic was so strong." She brushed the forelock from Indi's face. "Who are you, really?"

Big blue eyes watched her intently as his magic aura bloomed in bright colors. "*Pretty unicorn.*"

"Yes, you are. Beautiful."

"*I am for you, Emilee.*" Indi spun around, tapping his hooves, horn alight with sparkles.

"We killed those sea wolves and we could have killed many more. That's not what we are meant to do."

Indi nodded quickly.

"We're healers. We help," she explained gently.

"*I stay with you?*" Indi asked anxiously.

"I guess we're stuck with each other."

Indi nuzzled Emily. "*Stuck.*"

"But don't use magic unless I say so."

Indi danced across the deck, knocking Cribby over. "*I beautiful unicorn!*"

"I can see that, ya swarmy sea nut!"

"Are you all right?" Marlin asked, coming to sit beside her.

Emily nodded, leaning against a coil of rope.

For a while, the only sounds were the creak of the boat's timbers and the slap of the ocean's waves against its hull. Marlin got up and leaned over the side of the boat, staring into the ocean. "Niva's beneath us," he said after a while. "She says you saved her life—and the others', too."

Emily joined Marlin at the railing. Looking down, she saw a dark shape moving through the water. "You can really hear what she's thinking?"

"Maybe." Marlin's response was measured, but Emily could see the excitement sparking in his eyes.

"I thought you didn't have any magic," she whispered.

"I'm not a dragon rider." Marlin ran a hand through his hair. "Why did Niva rescue me?"

"I don't know. Some humans and animals are just meant to bond."

Marlin crossed his arms and glared at the horizon.

Giant green eyes lifted from the waves. Emily could swear the dragon wagged her tail.

She caught an image of Marlin on the dragon's back. "I think she wants you to ride her again," Emily said, glancing at the hopeful dragon.

Marlin recoiled like he'd been stung by a jellyfish. "No way!"

The dragon's eyelids drooped in disappointment as she sank dejectedly into the ocean.

A look of regret crossed Marlin's face.

"That was a very brave thing you did," she said.

"Yeah."

"You risked yourself to save Niva. You saved me back at Port Tuga, and you rescued Indi. I think you're in danger of becoming a real person."

He turned to Emily, fear in his eyes. "What's happened to me?"

Emily smiled. "You've bonded with Niva."

"But that's impossible!" Marlin wailed. "I've never bonded before."

"That makes two of us," Emily said, and sighed.

The sea dragon leaped up one last time, spraying the ship with water before vanishing back into the depths of the ocean.

"What should I do?" Marlin asked, suddenly worried.

"Have a little patience," she counseled.

Marlin slid to the deck, his back to the railing. "She's still sick."

"Easy." Emily knelt by his side. Beads of sweat dotted Marlin's face. Using her new power, she looked closer. Dim spots of red glowed around the merprince.

"All this sun has made me dizzy," Marlin said, frowning.

"Marlin . . ." Emily stammered. "You have the same sickness as the sea dragons."

"Ridiculous. I'm as healthy as a rock lobster," he scoffed. "Besides, I'm not magical."

"I can see your magical aura."

Marlin blushed a deep green. "Well then, fix me."

"I . . . can't, Marlin. I don't know exactly how."

The merboy sat for a minute, then quietly asked, "You're sure I have magic?"

Emily nodded. "I didn't think I was magical, either, at first."

"But I thought magic had pretty much vanished among our people, kept alive only by those stubborn dragon riders."

"It's not a curse, you know," Emily reminded him. "Magic is a gift."

"I don't know what to think."

"I think you really care," she said quietly.

"Do not," he muttered.

"You care so much, you're terrified. But when it comes down to what really matters, you'd do anything for your friends. That's what it's like to have a real bonded animal." She glanced at Indi, eating Cribby's hat.

"That's crazy." Marlin looked away, his mouth forming a sullen pout. "No one likes me."

"I do." Emily smiled shyly. "And Niva loves you."

"Truth is . . . I kinda like Niva," he admitted.

"I know."

The sun burned like a red ember as mist began billowing over the Flyer. Abruptly, the boat was shrouded by dense fog.

"Ack! This fog is thicker than me mum's chowder!" Cribby lit a wrought-iron lantern hanging from the mast. The bright light shone through the mist, illuminating dark shapes ghosting in and out of fog.

"I can't see a thing!" Marlin exclaimed.

"Do you know where we are?" Emily asked anxiously.

Cribby scratched his knobby head. "Of course I know where we are. We're right here!" He pointed a stubby finger at the chart. "Surrounded by deep waters, as far from land as—"

With a loud groan, the Flyer ground to a halt.

"Flibber me giblets!"

"Stuck," Indi said, peering over the side.

The Flyer was wedged between two gigantic rocks, caught in a stone vise.

Emily's breath caught. Broken masts, tattered sails, and pieces of wood littered the rocks like a junkyard. Skeletons lay sprawled across the rotting decks. They were trapped in a graveyard of lost ships.

"Hooweewee." Cribby whistled. "I gots a bad feeling about this."

Heavy mist hung over the water, making it impossible to see more than a few feet in front of them.

Beside her, Indi's horn pulsed in dark colors. Something was very wrong. Emily shivered as magic tingled around her.

"In an ocean of tears, we wait."

From the gloom, a lonely, singsong voice floated as if the ocean itself called to her.

"Waiting, longing for home."

Entranced by the achingly beautiful sound, homesickness washed over Emily. She suddenly missed Ozzie and her other friends terribly. How would they ever find her? She needed to go home.

"It's the most beautiful ting I ever heard," Cribby said, swaying back and forth, his eyes glassy as he stared into the rolling fog.

Another voice joined in the eerie melody, then another, building into an otherworldly chorus.

"Cribby, snap out of it!" Emily yelled.

Indi poked the elf captain in the rump.

"YeoWZir!" The elf covered his ears, eyes wide with sudden fear. "Sirens of the deep! They'll lure us in and drown us!"

"There is no today."

"No tomorrow."

"No place to go."

Spectral voices swept around them like ghosts. They seemed to be coming from everywhere at once.

"What do we do?" Marlin asked.

"Every seafaring elf knows how to protect himself from the siren's lure." Cribby leaped to the foredeck and started hopping around like a jumping bean. "Get wig-jiggy with it!"

The sea elf danced and spun, belting out his best pirate chantey.

> "O' me belt is a boot in a pirate's hat.
>   Swab the decks with a scurvy rat.
>   Yo, ho, ho and a bottle of—aK."

"Cribby?" Emily turned and gasped.

The sea elf was frozen like a statue. His mouth gaped like a fish, his eyes wide in terror.

"Marlin?"

Marlin stood stone still at the railing, spellbound. Someone was using powerful magic on them. Emily knew exactly what kind: spellsinging!

"Stay with us forever."

"It is time to come home."

She had never felt so homesick. Eyes half closed, she let the sweet melody fill the unbearable emptiness growing inside. "Where are you?"

"Come closer," the voices sang.

Iridescent sparkles passed under the surface. Something was moving toward her.

Reds, greens, blues, and oranges dazzled her eyes as shimmering fish-like bodies slinked past the boat. Wide tails flipped to the surface and slapped the water, then disappeared.

"Come to us."

Dreamily, Emily gazed into the water, cool mist brushing her face, washing away all her worries, all her cares.

The water was her element, her home. Emily wanted to be immersed in the eternal depths. "I want to go home," she said, not knowing if she spoke aloud.

Slowly, she climbed over the railing. She saw her reflection distorted in the black water. Then she saw other eyes staring at her. A beautiful face gazed at her from just below the surface. Cold, gleaming eyes, soulless and deep as the ocean itself, locked her in their spell.

Something wet and slimy slithered across Emily's ankle as long claws reached from the waters. Cold, webbed fingers slipped around her arms, pulling her into the icy depths.

"You belong to us now, witch."

Chapter 10

Emily knew she should be frightened as her feet silently slipped into the water.

"Come to us and slee—"

"—hooOOoop."

Through the watery surface, the creature's pale blue lips smiled reassuringly. Scales shimmered in the haze as slender hands reached for her. Emily barely felt their clawed fingers clasp her legs, dragging her down.

The spellsong washed over her with the endless rhythm of the ocean, calling her home.

"The ocean is your ho—"

"—bLaaaaaRRrrp!"

Her eyes drooped as she drifted away, slowly lowering herself overboard. The dream would last forever; she never wanted to come bac—

"—aAKKKKKKK!" A blaring noise suddenly cut through the spell. Emily's eyes flew open and she screamed, grasping desperately for the boat railing.

The creatures thrashed and hissed like snakes. Iridescent hair of pale green, blue, and amber swayed with their every move. Glistening tails caught the sunlight as cold eyes reflected the blues and greens of the ocean.

Mermaids!

They were everywhere, slender, scaly bodies shimmering like ghosts in the water.

A mermaid floated upon the surface, pale lips covering rows of serrated teeth. Glittering eyes gazed out of a beautiful doll-like face. Emily could make out the unmistakable red aura of the water sickness shimmering around the mermaid.

"You cannot escape." The mermaid's voice was sharp as a knife, nothing like the gentle melody of the enchanting song.

"PhoOOoof!"

A pink and purple unicorn muzzle pressed over the rail close to Emily's face, horn shining bright.

The mermaids snarled and shrank back from Indi's magic.

Emily grabbed on to her bonded's neck as he pulled her from the water. She fell on the deck in a heap, scrambling away from the creatures. In a few seconds she would have been pulled under.

"FlooT! wHarK!" Indi honked wildly, shattering the last of the spell that held Marlin and Cribby.

The prince stared, openmouthed, at the wild creatures. "I don't believe it!"

"I think it's working," Cribby said, stomping madly around the deck. He looked over the side and blanched. "Clam almighty!"

Marlin grabbed Emily's arm, pulling her away from the railing. "Wild mermaids! Look, they still have tails! It's so primitive."

Emily gulped. "You mean you've never seen a real mermaid before?"

"No." He shook his head. "Have you?"

"No."

A blue-haired mermaid rose from the depths, gleaming eyes locked on Emily. "You bring darkness upon us."

"I'm a healer," Emily protested.

"You will kill us all," another mermaid hissed.

Emily flashed on her dark visions—so many animals trapped in her web, their magic ripped away by her power.

"It was an accident." Emily shrank back from the angry creature, ashamed. "I didn't mean to hurt anyone."

"You can talk!" Marlin stared at the mermaids, astonished.

"Great prince."

Dozens of ice-cold eyes turned to Marlin.

"You are the one."

"Who, me?" Marlin goggled, shying away.

"You saved the sea dragon," a mermaid said.

"Word travels fast," he said.

"Talk to them," Emily urged.

"I don't speak fish."

Cribby pushed the merboy forward. "Stop floundering."

The mermaids swarmed around the boat. "We knew you would come, Prince. But why do you bring the dark witch?"

"She will destroy us," another hissed.

Emily's heart pounded. It was an *accident*—wasn't it?

"What do you want from me?" Marlin asked.

The mermaids' shimmering scales trailed magic in the dark water.

"You shall be a great king of legend and restore the magic of the oceans."

"We have foreseen it."

"Hey, did you hear that?" Marlin beamed at Emily. "I'm going to be famous."

Emily stepped forward cautiously. "I—we want to heal the sea creatures."

"You cannot," the mermaid snarled.

Emily shrank back.

"The water magic is making us sick," another mermaid wailed.

"The water magic?" Emily repeated.

Of course! That's why all the animals were infected. The virus was in the water itself. Panic raced along her spine. She couldn't travel to the source of every stream, river, and lake—it would take forever. Healing the water would require elemental magic way beyond her abilities.

"No problem," Marlin proclaimed, suddenly full of confidence. Then he turned to Emily. "How do we do that?"

"You must use great magic, merprince," a mermaid told Marlin. "Find the Crystal Caves."

Maybe this wouldn't be impossible after all, Emily thought.

"The Crystal Caves don't exist." Marlin snorted. "They're a child's fairy tale!"

Emily's heart sank. "Great."

Then something tickled in the back of her mind. Emily turned to Indi. She had seen a place—a place with hundreds of magic jewels.

"*Magic.*" Indi nodded.

"Marlin, I think they do exist," Emily said, sheepishly. "I saw them . . . in a vision."

"That's silly."

"No," she insisted. "There must be a power crystal there twisting all the water magic."

Marlin eyed the mermaids. "If the water magic is bad, why can't you go fix it yourselves?"

"We are bound to this place."

"You mean you're trapped here?" Emily asked.

Marlin smiled brightly at the mermaids. "I officially decree you're free to go."

"There is nowhere left for us." The mermaids looked away, eyes glistening with pain. "We are all that remain."

Emily couldn't help thinking of what it must have been like once upon a time, when incredible creatures like sea dragons and these mermaids filled the world.

"You must help us find this magic," the healer pleaded. "Please."

"Such power is not safe in your hands," the mermaid told her scornfully.

Emily was stunned.

"You really saw this place?" Marlin asked Emily.

She and Indi nodded.

"And you think there's a power crystal there?"

"It would make sense for one to be drawn to all that magic."

The merprince took a deep breath and spoke to the mermaids. "If I promise to heal the water magic, you must let us all go, including the, um, witch."

The mermaids scowled. "She belongs to the sea."

"I am the great merking and I won't leave without her."

The mermaids swam in a tight circle, blue, amber, and green hair swirling in a gleaming cloud.

"You shall all be free, but heed our warning."

"How do we find the Crystal Caves?" Marlin asked.

"Behind the Rainbow Veil you will find what you are looking for."

"The Rainbow Veil?" Emily repeated.

"The moon and sun will show you the way." Ice-cold eyes locked on Emily's. "Be warned, witch, the darkness is upon you."

Goosebumps prickled along Emily's arms as the mermaids slipped silently beneath the waters and vanished.

"Nobody's goin' nowheres, mermatey," Cribby whispered hoarsely.

"Why's that?" Marlin asked.

The elf leaped to his feet. "Because, ya scrub-wheel, we're held fast in these rocks!"

But suddenly, a thick mist blew across the deck, setting the Flyer free from the mermaid's spell.

"Avast!" Cribby grabbed the wheel.

Through the rolling fog, flashing lights began swirling, faster and faster. The water around the Flyer surged, catching the boat in a whirlpool. In its churning center, pearly blue and green magic crackled as a shimmering portal swirled open.

"I hope you know what you're doing," Marlin called out.

"Me too." Emily hugged Indi close.

The unicorn looked at her with eyes full of trust. Suddenly Emily had what she had always wanted: a bonded animal. But it wasn't at all as she'd imagined. Instead of stronger magic for healing, she had accidentally used her powerful magic to hurt—even kill—animals.

The mermaids' words were a chilling reminder of what Miranda had told her: Her magic would only cause pain.

Chapter 11

"I'll be a mage's monkey!" Cribby exclaimed, turning his charts upside down. "We're halfway up the Snake River!"

The Fearless Flyer floated through dense jungle. Along the banks, thick vines curled into the swift waters. Colorful birds swept through moss laden trees.

"The mermaids were guarding a portal." Marlin shielded his eyes from the sudden sunlight dancing over the deck. "How weird is that?"

Emily shot the merprince an exasperated look.

Marlin raised his hands in defense. "I'm still new to this magic stuff. I guess it can get plenty weird."

"Honk." Indi pranced across the deck.

"You have no idea," Emily muttered. When it came to magic, weird was only the beginning.

"Onward to the Crystal Caves, Captain Cribby," Marlin called to the sea elf.

Cribby shuddered. "We'll never survive to tell the tale."

"What makes you say that?" Emily asked.

"Anyone who's ever tried has never been seen, heard from, or sung of again. Just a final painful shriek and then—ArK."

"What?"

"ArrRRkkKK!" Cribby repeated loudly.

"Oh." Marlin shook his head.

"We can heal the water magic there, I know it," Emily insisted adamantly.

"And jus' what ye be lookin' fer in these caves?" Cribby asked in a hushed tone.

"Jewels," she said. "Hundreds of them."

"Merman the mainsail!"

Marlin pulled the rigging tight, sending the Flyer leaning into the wind.

Emily gazed down the river as it curved out of sight. Fear wormed its way into her heart. Would she be able to heal the water magic without hurting anyone else?

Indi pressed close to Emily's side, sensing her worry. *"We make magic together."*

She leaned against Indi's soft fur. She wasn't alone anymore. No matter what happened, her bonded was there to help her.

When this was over they'd have all the time they needed to grow together and work on their magic. She couldn't wait to show him the forests of Ravenswood. He was going to love it there with all the other magical animals—although she'd have to be careful. Her mom would faint if she saw a pink and purple unicorn poking around the Pet Palace! There was so much they had to look forward to, all the things she had longed to do when she finally bonded with an animal.

"It's not just sea dragons, is it?" Marlin asked, breaking her thoughts.

Emily shook her head.

"The whole ocean is in danger, my entire kingdom." Realization filled the merteen's eyes with sadness. "I was taught to prepare for a world without magic. Then, I find Niva, you find Indi, *and* we bump into *real* mermaids. I don't know anything anymore."

"You can't deny what you are, Marlin," Emily told him. "You're connected to the water and its magic. You always were."

"Yeah, next you're going to tell me Avalon really exists," he scoffed. When Emily didn't smile, he continued. "If Avalon were real, magic wouldn't be disappearing, would it?"

"When my friends and I saved Aldenmor, we released a lot of magic from somewhere." Emily turned away, Miranda's words haunting her. "Now, that magic is running wild. If we don't find nine power crystals, and get them back in time, that magic could wind up in the hands of terrible people."

"If you can classify the Spider Witch and the Dark Sorceress as 'people,'" Marlin quipped. "What do these nine crystals do?"

"I'm not sure exactly. But they're unstable and very dangerous, powerful enough to twist magic itself."

"How many have you got so far?" the merprince asked.

"Four, but one was destroyed. So that's five more to go."

"But if you've destroyed one, you'll never get enough."

Emily had no answer for that.

"You think there's one in the crystal caves?" Marlin asked.

"Yes."

"And it's twisting the water magic."

Emily nodded.

"Well, what do we do with them once we collect them all?"

"I don't know," Emily admitted.

Marlin shook his head. "Geez, nobody really seems to know anything about magic."

"Some things are worth fighting for—even if they seem impossible," Emily said quietly.

"I turned my back on magic, and now the dragons could become extinct because of me."

"No, Marlin," she said, looking into his eyes. "They're dying because the magic is sick. And if what the mermaids said is true, you must help them. And Niva."

"I . . ." Marlin cast his eyes down. "Emily, I don't know what to do."

"You can protect the magic that's left before it's too late."

"Truth is, the merkingdom needs a warrior, a dragon rider, not me. I don't deserve to be heir," he said in a small voice.

Underneath all his snobbiness and arrogance, Marlin was just scared of failing, afraid of disappointing his people. She understood that better than anyone.

"I didn't choose to be a healer," Emily said. "But I am. We have to do the best we can with what's given to us."

Marlin gazed at her, his brown eyes softening as he smiled.

"Need some help here, mateys!" Cribby called. "These sails ain't gonna trim themselves."

"Okay." Marlin slapped his knees and stood up, offering a hand to Emily. "Let's go get a power crystal and save the world."

"Heading forty degrees port," Cribby directed.

Emily got to her feet and looked ahead. They had come to a fork in the river. One branch continued through more jungle. The other branch churned into ominous dark canyons.

She felt magic tickling up and down her arms, pulling her forward.

"*Magic,*" Indi said, and pointed his horn toward the canyons.

"We have to go that way," Emily called to Cribby.

"Don't be absurd, ya muckwiggle," the elf protested. "That river ain't even on the charts."

"That's where we have to go."

"You heard her, turn this boat," Marlin ordered.

The sea elf grumbled. "That'll teach me for ferrying a mage, a merprince and a . . ." Cribby looked at Indi. "What kind of a beastie are you?"

"Most beautiful unicorn on web," Indi tooted.

"Yeah, well, would ye mind tootin' over yonder." The captain pushed Indi aside, pulling the ropes tightly over the supply barrels. "Gonna be a rough ride. Winds are fierce through these canyons."

The Flyer bobbed like a top as it passed into the shadows of the sheer canyons. Caves pockmarked the cliff walls like dark eyes watching.

Emily stood beneath the mast, Indi by her side. She flushed as Marlin hovered protectively close. Swirling whirlpools shot geysers spiraling high in the air. The twisting waters cascaded over them, covering the Flyer with spray.

"It ain't all tweetybirds and pretty monkeys out there," Cribby warned, hunching behind the wheel.

"No?" Marlin asked.

"Nohoho!" the elf grimaced. "There's monsters bigger than yer house lurkin'. Lurkin', I tell ya!"

"Monsters?" Emily shivered.

The sun sank behind thick clouds, sending shifting pools of inky shadows over the wooden deck. The wind was a constant sigh, like the whispering of ghosts.

"Great beasties with claws that could rrrrrrrrip ye to pieces!" Cribby continued. "And big teeth that could rrrrrrrrrr—"

A loud noise clanked behind the cabin.

Emily stopped short. Something was hiding in the darkness on the other side of the boat!

Indi stepped in front of Emily, horn glowing with bright colors.

Marlin's hand slid to his knife hilt.

A shadow grew across the foredeck, taking the shape of a huge figure, arms raised with long claws.

"Unhand that mage!" a deep voice boomed.

"What the—" Cribby stuttered, falling over his sandals.

"Who's there?" Marlin called out.

"I be the dreaded pirate of—"

A series of whispers followed.

"What?"

"The dreaded pirate of Dingly Dell!"

"Oh, no!" Cribby gasped. "Who?"

"Unhand the mage, or face the wrath of the great beast of—"

Marlin and Emily looked at each other.

Another shadow rose over the deck: a huge, four-legged creature, hunched and ready to spring.

"The great beast with big teeth!" the voice called out.

"The mage is unharmed." Marlin raised his hands. "You are making a mistake."

"It is you who have made the mistake, sir!"

With a shake of his head, Indi's horn lit up like a spotlight, piercing the shadows. There on the deck stood a golden brown ferret and a large, spotted cat.

"I laugh, I scoff, I—*gah!*" Ozzie jumped back into the shadows.

"Ozzie!" Emily ran to the ferret. Scooping him up in her arms, she hugged him tight. "You're okay!"

"Can't—breathe—!"

"Lyra!" Emily embraced the cat, squashing the ferret against Lyra's side.

"*Are you all right?*" Lyra nuzzled tears off Emily's face.

"I'm fine," the healer cried. "I'm just so glad to see you."

"Ferret—is—being—squeezed!"

"*Whoohoo—oop.*" Indi pranced across the deck, bumping into Emily's legs.

"All right." Ozzie scrambled from Emily's arms, glaring at Cribby and Marlin. "What's going on here? Did you kidnap her?"

"No!"

"No!"

"*Honk!*"

"Oh, well. All right, then"—Ozzie petted the strange unicorn standing beside him—"and who's this handsome creature?"

"He ate my jewel," Emily said.

"Gah!" Ozzie kicked Indi's foreleg.

"How did you find me?" the healer asked.

"You're welcome." Ozzie puffed up his chest.

"Where are the others?

"Um—somewhere between portals."

Emily was suddenly concerned again. "Are they all right?

"They're—" Ozzie looked around. "It's a long story."

"We tried to contact you, but couldn't get through." Lyra examined Indi up and down.

"I locked on to your jewel," Ozzie explained. "We tried to follow it and we got caught in your magic. The others got tossed."

Emily had hurt her friends, and now they were lost because of her magic. "I tried to cure the sea animals and it got out of control and—"

"It's okay," Lyra purred.

"Great beasts!" Cribby yelled, finally finding his voice. "A flying cat and a talking weasel!"

"That's Lyra, and this is Ozzie," Emily introduced her friends.

"Hey, it's you again," Marlin said.

Ozzie marched up to the prince. "If you've touched one hair on this mage, I'll—"

"Ozzie," Emily said, pulling the ferret back by his tail. "It's okay. Marlin's a friend."

"Humph!"

Suddenly Ozzie slid to the prow as the Flyer plunged into a swell of choppy water. Emily grabbed the wooden railing, stumbling as the small boat pitched into the rapids.

Ozzie squeezed in between Emily and Indi. "So, anyway, I was blown somewhere in the middle of the ocean and this big dumb turtle—"

"Hey, guys?" Lyra tried to break in.

"Not now, in a second—" Ozzie waved at the cat. "Adriane and Kara couldn't just jump through one portal. Nooooooo, they had to jump though four!"

The rapids churned and roiled, getting stronger and stronger. Foam sprayed the deck as the craft dipped in the swirling waters.

"Guys!" Lyra tried to break in again. *"There's a huge—"*

"Hey, what's that noise?" Ozzie asked suddenly.

The mighty boom rumbled across the river, rattling the small boat.

"Avast!" Cribby frantically spun the wheel as the noise turned to a deep thudding.

Ahead of them a wall of foam sprayed skyward and—where was the river? It just seemed to vanish.

The roar of pounding water filled their ears.

"Um . . . what is that?" Ozzie squeaked.

"It's a giant waterfall, ya fish-tongued sea weasel!"

"GAH!"

"Hang on!" Marlin clung to the railing as the Flyer plunged forward.

Indi planted his hooves wide apart on the deck, steadying himself and Emily.

Oh no! I must have made a mistake, Emily thought, clutching Indi with one hand, Ozzie with the other.

"Turn the ship around!" Cribby screamed, but it was too late.

There was a moment of weightlessness as the prow hung over the falls, suspended on the crest—

Emily's stomach lurched as the ship pitched forward. She was looking straight down at least twenty-five stories! Foam and spray crashed against the rocks below.

With a final shudder, the Flyer plummeted over the waterfall.

"Skagawagger!"

Chapter 12

Everyone screamed as the Fearless Flyer plunged straight toward the jagged rocks below.

Emily clung to the mast as Ozzie rolled across the deck, crashing into Lyra's side.

Abruptly, the boat lurched, slowing its rapid descent—as if someone put on the brakes—in mid-air!

"What's going on?" Marlin yelled, gripping the rail.

The river tilted and spun beneath them as the boat swung away from the waterfall. The Flyer was living up to its name. It was flying!

A large shadow swept across the deck, followed by a great rush of wind. Emily felt the dragon's immense strength even before she saw him. "Drake!"

Drake swooped from the sky, Adriane, Zach, and Dreamer on his back. Bands of silver and red magic lassoed the boat, lifting it up and away from the falls.

"Drake, take us down easy," Zach called out.

"I am trying." Muscles corded like iron along the

dragon's neck as mighty wings skimmed the outer edges of the falls.

Orange light crackled wildly.

"I can't swim!" Ozzie suddenly remembered, focusing his ferret stone. The air around him responded to his power, a heavy surge that pushed the boat away from the tangle of sharp rocks.

With a roar, Drake lowered the Flyer into calmer waters, splashing the already soaked crew. The boat settled in a mossy alcove a safe distance away from the thundering waterfall.

Drake landed on the prow, tipping the vessel deep in the mud.

"Dragon!" Cribby cried, terrified.

A quick hand signal from Adriane sent Dreamer leaping from the dragon's back. The black mistwolf pinned Cribby to the deck, lips pulled back in a fearsome snarl.

"Clam almighty!"

"Emily!" Adriane slid off Drake and swept up her friend in a hug.

Zach leaped aboard the Flyer. "Don't move!" he ordered Cribby.

"No, wait! He's a friend." Emily pulled the mistwolf away. "This is Captain Cribby."

"Garg, he's too bulky, man!" Cribby sprang up, trying to push the enormous dragon off the boat.

"And Prince Marlin."

Adriane scowled at the merboy before turning to Emily. "Are you sure you're okay?"

"I can't believe you guys found me!" Emily was laughing and crying all at once.

Zach eased Marlin back. "You don't look so good."

"Yeah, thanks for the rescue," the prince said, staring in awe at the Drake.

Ozzie marched over, indignant. "About time you showed up!" he yelled at the big, red dragon.

"Now what's going on?" Adriane asked.

Marlin, Emily, Indi, Cribby, and Ozzie started talking at once.

"We got swept away and—"

"All of a sudden we were on—"

"—beautiful unicorn."

"—a big, dumb turtle!"

"—with bulwoggles and mermaids!"

"—hobnobbler!"

"One at a time!" Adriane yelled.

Dreamer sniffed Indi, catching the warrior's eye.

"A unicorn," Adriane exclaimed. "He's so cute!"

"He ate my jewel."

Dreamer growled.

"Fine." Adriane threw up her hands. "Join the party."

"Did somebody say 'party'?"

Another winged shadow swept over the boat.

"Kara!" Emily waved as Nightwing landed next to Drake, pitching the Flyer forward.

"Good gob, man!" Cribby wailed. "Are ya batty?"

Emily ran to the blond girl, catching her as she dismounted. "I'm so glad to see you."

"Ditto." Kara brushed herself off, smiling as if she had just arrived at a school dance. "What a beautiful waterfall. Did you guys see that?"

"No," Adriane said, straight-faced. "Which one are you talking about?"

"That one." The blazing star pointed. "It's ginormous!"

"We ended up over the jungles, and Nightwing tracked you here," Lorren explained.

Indi pranced up to Kara, showing off his dazzling horn.

"Ooo, what a cute unic—"

"He ate Emily's jewel," Ozzie informed her, ferret arms crossed.

"Gross."

"He's bonded to me," Emily said shyly.

"Stuck." Indi danced around proudly, coming nose-to-nose with Ozzie.

"All righty, then." Kara clapped her hands. "Time to wrap this up and go home."

"Kara," Emily said, patting Indi's head. "We think we know where the power crystal is. We can't turn back now."

"Girls." Kara draped her arms around Adriane

and Emily. "In case no one's noticed, it's half past our show-up-at-home-before-we-get-busted time."

"Where's Tasha?" Lorren asked. "She's got the jewel locator; she should have been here first."

"She'll find us," Kara said.

"Maybe she got thrown into another portal," Zach suggested.

"We have to press on," Marlin said. "Too many lives are at stake."

"Listen, pal." Lorren stepped close to Marlin. "I'm not leaving here without her!"

Emily caught a momentary flare of jealousy in Kara's eyes.

"Okay." Marlin backed off.

Lorren turned to the group and sighed. "Sorry. It's just that Tasha and I . . . we've been friends since we were little. I promised her family I would look out for her when she entered the court."

"There's nothing to be sorry about," Kara said.

Lorren turned away to watch the river. "We don't even know where we are."

"We were led here," Emily explained. "To find magic and heal the water."

"Who would lead you over a waterfall?" Adriane exclaimed.

Cribby snorted. "I'd like to meet the soddy sea salt that would follow them orders."

They all looked at the sea captain.

"Mermaids," Marlin said.

"Mermaids?" Kara repeated.

Emily sighed. "There's a lot to tell."

"Fine, what have you got to eat around here?" Ozzie started rummaging through supplies and utensils strewn about the deck.

"We gots . . ." The sea elf picked up a barrel that didn't look broken. "Grainnubs and some bread."

"Well, I suppose I could cook a nubwhich," Ozzie mused. "Who's hungry?"

Drake's roar echoed up and down the river.

Adriane was at the dragon's side in a flash, soothing her big baby boy. "Ozzie, make about fifty for Drake."

"Okay, you!" Kara took Emily by the hand and sat her on the steps of the cabin. "Tell us everything. With details."

Emily blushed.

"Just Emily." Adriane turned the eager ferret around.

Soon smoke wafted from the galley as Ozzie whipped up snacks. Drake sat on the grassy bank, hovering over the group protectively as Emily explained the events that had led her to the Snake River. It was strange to have the other mages hanging on to her every word. Usually Emily was the one who listened to everyone else's adventures.

"We're supposed to find the Rainbow Veil that leads to the Crystal Caves," she concluded.

"And now you have, like, magic X-ray vision?" Kara asked eagerly. "Quick, does my aura match my outfit?"

Adriane pushed to her feet. "Emily, when your magic hit us, it was really strong."

Emily gently stroked Dreamer and Lyra. "I'm so sorry."

Both animals leaned against the healer protectively.

"Indi eating your jewel explains Tasha's reading," Kara mused. "But then what happened?"

"I tried to heal all the animals. But I couldn't control it," Emily said quietly. "So many animals were caught in my magic. And . . ."

They waited for her to continue.

"I was hurting them. . . ." Emily's eyes watered.

Adriane and Kara exchanged a worried glance.

"But somehow Indi brought me out of it."

"You can thank me later," Ozzie called out.

"You woke him up?" Emily asked Ozzie.

"I connected with your jewel, and since he swallowed it, well, you do the math."

Emily gave Ozzie a big kiss on his furry head.

"Or you can thank me now."

"I think there's a power crystal in the caves," Emily continued. "And it's poisoning the water magic—"

"Wait a minute," Kara said to Emily. "I needed

almost everyone's help when I created my magic network of friends."

"Yeah, how *did* you use so much power?" Ozzie asked Emily as he eyed Indi up and down. "Even if this—"

"Pretty unicorn."

"Whatever—is bonded to you."

They all looked at the healer.

She didn't know how to explain the rest, so she said in a rush, "Okay, I think I met a wizard."

The group gasped.

"Rewind," Adriane ordered.

Emily shook her head. It was as if pieces of her memory were just blanked out.

"Er, the merprince and meeself dun remember seein' no wizard," Cribby chimed in.

"Obviously you were under some kind of spell." Adriane turned to Marlin and Cribby accusingly.

"Darned dangled magic," Cribby grumbled.

"This wizard knew about us," Emily continued. "She said the magic we released to save Aldenmor didn't come from Avalon. . . ."

"How would she know?" Adriane asked.

Emily shrugged. "She said it was her magic."

"Whoa, that's crazy." Kara shook her head.

"But here we are. I know the answer's in the Crystal Caves," Emily insisted.

"So how do we find this veil?" Zach paced up and

down the deck, hands clasped behind his back, deep in thought.

"It could be anywhere." Kara leaned over the railing, absently swinging her unicorn jewel. "With magic, always expect the unexpected."

"Tell me about it," Marlin griped.

"You got a month?" Kara's pink jewel sparkled as it caught the rays of the setting sun.

Emily's eyes widened. "Look at that."

"Huh? Oh yeah, my jewel is too cool."

Emily jumped to her feet. "Do that again."

"What?"

"With your jewel."

Kara caught the sunlight again. Sparkles of light splashed across the waterfall as rainbow colors shimmered in the billowing mist.

Everyone rushed toward Kara.

"Oh, now I'm popular again," she quipped.

"There it is!" Marlin grasped the railing, mouth agape.

Rainbow colors shimmered under the cloud of mist illuminating—

"—The Rainbow Veil!" Emily exclaimed.

Kara played with the lights from her jewel. "It must be a secret door."

"But how do we open it?" Adriane asked.

"Booty or no booty, the falls would smash mee wee boot to pieces!" Cribby cried.

Emily cocked her head, studying the falls. She knew Cribby was right, but the mermaids said they had to go *behind* the Rainbow Veil.

"The sun and the moon will show you the way. . . ." Emily repeated the line under her breath.

"Your jewel is catching the rays of the setting sun," Adriane pointed out to Kara.

The red orange sphere melted over the western skies, sending beams through Kara's jewel.

"Dee light!" Cribby shouted.

"Yes, it is very pretty," Ozzie agreed.

"Dee light from dee moon!" Cribby pointed.

In the east, twin moons were rising, silver orbs hanging in the sky. In a few seconds both sun and moons would be in perfect balance across the heavens.

But Cribby was pointing now at Adriane's jewel.

The wolf stone glowed bright silver.

Adriane angled her jewel to catch the moonlight. Deep silvery blue magic shimmered like a starry night sky across the waterfall.

"The sun and the moon will show you the way!" Emily exclaimed, as understanding dawned.

Adriane glanced at Kara. For once, they were in synch. Powered by the sun and moon, their jewels glowed bright silver and pink. Water sprayed everywhere as the power of night and day collided in the center of the falls, crackling like fireworks.

But the veil did not open.

They needed something to balance them, to make them work together—or, in this case, apart.

The healer stepped forward, Indi by her side, and took her familiar position between the others. Adriane and Dreamer stood to her left, Kara and Lyra to her right. Emily felt balanced, Indi's magic steadying her.

Reaching out, she raised her hands, one facing the light and one the dark. A tiny rainbow shimmered in the center of the veil, expanding as Emily drew on Kara and Adriane's magic. The rainbow widened, parting the mist like a curtain.

"You did it!" Kara exclaimed.

"Even without your jewel," Adriane observed, impressed.

"With Indi." Emily smiled as her bonded pranced beside her.

"Clamdoodle!" Cribby skipped like a rugrat.

"We have to hurry." Kara's jewel had lost some of its brilliance as the sun and moon shifted in the skies. The curtain was beginning to close.

"Let's go!" Marlin yelled as the others scurried into motion.

"What about Tasha?" Lorren asked.

"We can't wait, Lorren," Emily said.

"She'll find us," Kara said, her voice strained but steady. "She has the locator."

"Drake, we need you to wait here for Tasha," Zach said, patting the dragon's side.

Adriane planted a kiss on the dragon's wide nose. "Love you."

"Be careful, Mama."

"I will."

With a nudge from Drake's head, the Flyer slid from its muddy berth.

The rushing roar of the falls engulfed the boat as they approached the magical doorway.

"Everyone stay sharp," Adriane ordered. "If there's a power crystal in there, we have to be ready for anything."

Water churned up and over them as the Flyer entered the open veil.

"My hair is going to be a frizzy mess," Kara shouted. "Good thing I know magic."

"I see light ahead," Marlin cried.

Rumbling thunder threatened to shake the Flyer apart as the waterfall crashed closer and closer on either side of the boat.

"We're almost through!" Cribby said, dancing from foot to foot.

"Hurry!" Zach called out.

The Flyer broke through the final layer of mist. With a resounding boom, the veil closed behind them.

"We made it!"

The group was thrown forward as the horrendous sound of splintering wood and metal screeched through the air.

"Ferret overboard!" Ozzie screamed, sliding across the deck, paws flailing.

"Hang on." Lyra darted in front of him.

Gasping for air, Emily wiped the mist from her eyes. "Oh no," she breathed.

The boat ground to a halt, tilting sharply. Snagged on sharp rocks, a gaping hole ripped along its side. This time, the Fearless Flyer had found its final resting place.

Chapter 13

"Oh, the mermanatee!" Cribby cried as Lorren and Zach dragged the sea elf off the boat.

The group huddled in a wide grotto, staring at what was left of the Fearless Flyer.

Tattered sails drooped from the broken mast, draping the wreckage like a shroud.

"Maybe we can fix it," Zach suggested hopefully.

WhoomPH! The Flyer collapsed like a house of cards, leaving only a pile of splintered debris.

Cribby fell to his knees, sobbing.

"I'm sorry about the Flyer," Emily said. "She was a good . . . boot."

"None like her!" Cribby wailed.

"If we make it back to Aquatania, we'll build you a new one," Marlin promised.

Cribby sniffled. "With a bilge pump?"

"Yeah."

"And a poop deck?"

"Yes, yes, whatever. Now let's get moving."

Dappled blue light filtered through the waterfall, dimly illuminating a cavern of dull brown rock. Behind them, the falls thundered down, an impenetrable wall of water. Before them a small lake reflected sparkling light from its glassy surface.

"These are the Crystal Caves?" Marlin's disappointed voice echoed along the curving walls.

Emily's heart sank. Where were the magic jewels she had seen in her vision? Had she come all this way for nothing? "The Rainbow Veil *must* be guarding something," the healer insisted.

Taking a deep breath, she rested her hand on Indi's silky neck and closed her eyes. Focusing deep into the cavern's gloom, she searched for the magic. Indi leaned close, supporting her, his aura shining bright purple and blue. Suddenly a swirling emerald light wavered in the distance.

Indi nosed his horn toward the far side of the cavern. *"That way."*

"There's something on the other side of this lake," Emily said.

"Dreamer, check it out," Adriane ordered.

The mistwolf padded down a narrow path skirting the lake.

"What gives?" Kara looked at the eerily calm grotto. "Power crystals always create chaos. Shouldn't there be some magical craziness, some sign of total pandemonium, some—"

Dreamer's howl echoed in the cavern. *"Magic."*

"This way." Adriane moved stealthily down the narrow pathway around the lake.

The group followed, jewels raised and ready.

"Are you all right?" Emily glanced at Marlin's strained face.

"Yeah."

She rested her hand against the merprince's cheek. "You're burning up. You have to rest."

"I'll be okay."

"What's wrong with him?" Lorren called out.

"Maybe he has the flooie," Kara suggested.

"It's the water sickness," Emily explained.

"Don't worry, it's not contagious unless you have a fin or two," Marlin said, chuckling.

Zach walked beside the merboy. "You need some help?"

"No, thank you." Marlin smiled weakly. "Hey, when this is all over, you guys all have to come to the Wave Fest; it's a great party—really."

"Beach parties are the best!" Kara agreed.

"Mmm, clam-on-a-stick." Ozzie smacked his lips.

"Your father seemed pretty upset with the dragon riders," Lorren reminded the merprince.

"He'll have to get over it." Marlin raised his head high. "I was wrong about the dragon riders. And I'm sorry to all of you for everything. I . . . just didn't know any better."

"Join the club." Zach slapped him on the back.

"What about the sea dragons?" Adriane asked.

"That's Emily's department," Marlin said. "She's the best healer I know."

Emily glanced back. "I'm the only healer you know."

The group encircled Marlin, keeping him steady.

Emily followed Indi, her senses tingling. There was powerful magic ahead. But what if it wasn't enough? What if she still couldn't heal the water magic? Everyone was counting on her to fix the oceans and save the sea dragons.

Emerald eyes gleaming, Dreamer appeared in front of them. *"In there."*

Silvery blue light glowed faintly, just enough for them to see an opening in the cavern wall. Tiny crystals littered the floor, sparkling like stars.

"Okay, everyone into the creepy tunnel." Kara pushed Lorren and Adriane in front of her.

Once inside, the tunnel narrowed—soon they could only pass single file. Adriane, Zach, and Dreamer took the lead, followed by Emily, Marlin, and Indi. Kara, Lorren, Lyra, and a despondent Cribby brought up the rear. Their shuffling footsteps echoed as the sound of the falls faded away.

The tunnel's walls seemed to close in around her. Emily shuddered.

"Hope there's nothing living in here," Ozzie said, grimacing as he sidestepped puddles of brackish water.

"Are there any beasties we *haven't* seen yet?" Cribby cried out.

"Manticore," Adriane offered.

"Demons," Zach continued.

"Werebeasts," Lorren said.

"Bedbugs," Kara added.

"Criminy!" Cribby held his hands to his ears.

Suddenly Indi raised his horn. Magic swirled in bright rainbow colors.

"Magic, dead ahead," Adriane announced as the group barreled into one another.

Wolf, unicorn, dragon, and ferret gems sparkled brightly, reflecting light from the broad opening.

Emily's breath caught as they entered another hidden cavern. Glowing stalactites hung from the arched ceiling, shimmering in shades of silver. Water fell behind crystal walls, sending patterns of light waving across the cave.

Kara followed Lorren out of the tunnel, eyes wide. "Wow."

It was like they had stepped into the middle of a shining rainbow. Hundreds of giant jewels twinkled on the cavern floor, pulsing and sparkling with magic.

"We found it." Emily smiled, her eyes locked on the luminous, basketball-sized jewels. Beautiful green, turquoise, and silver auras swirled around the gems in twisting patterns, exactly as she had seen in her vision. Indi nuzzled close, his horn reflecting brilliant prisms of light.

"This is amazing!" Kara twirled around, taking in the wondrous magic.

"Yeah," Adriane agreed. "It's—"

"Bootyful!" Cribby slid across the slick floor, diving into a pile of jewels. "Look a' the size a' these mammas!" He hugged armfuls of glittering gems.

Zach picked a particularly large one up in his hands, turning it over slowly.

Cribby's eyes opened wide. "I'll be rich! Rich, I say, with more magic than I can waggle a wand at!"

Adriane studied the swirling colors carefully. "These look familiar."

"There's something very peculiar about these jewels," Ozzie said, sizing up several dozen that were bigger than he was.

"These aren't jewels," Zach announced.

Everyone looked at the blond teen.

"They're eggs."

Chapter 14

"**D**ragons!" Zach exclaimed, smiling in wonder. "There must be hundreds of them."

"What the—!" Ozzie hopped away from the multicolored eggs.

Adriane knelt beside Dreamer. "They're smaller than the egg Drake came from, but the markings are similar."

Colors swirled as the warrior's hand passed over the eggs.

"Ooo, they come in fuchsia." Kara picked up a glorious, pink egg.

"Wow," Emily gasped.

"What?" Kara asked.

At the blazing star's touch, the egg's shifting aura brightened to gleaming gold.

"I wish you could see their magic. It's incredible." Emily stretched her arms wide, letting the dragon magic wash over her—bright halos, sparkling and pure. "They're totally healthy."

"No trace of the water sickness?" Marlin asked anxiously.

"None," Emily confirmed, glancing at the merboy. The red glow in his aura had dimmed. The eggs definitely had a healing effect on the water virus.

"How are you feeling?" she asked.

"Amazing! Actually," Marlin answered.

"This magic is helping you," Emily said with a smile. "I can see it."

"I don't sense a power crystal here," Adriane observed, her wolf stone lying coolly on her bracelet.

Ozzie frowned. "If there's no power crystal twisting the magic, then where is the sickness coming from?"

Emily didn't have an answer.

Lorren shook his head, amazed. "Zach, how long do you think these have been here?"

"From what I've learned, dragon eggs can gestate for thousands of years." Zach carefully examined a pile. "There are—well, there used to be—all kinds of dragons."

"Wyverns, which walk on two legs," Adriane said.

"Flying dragons," Dreamer chimed in.

"Dragonflies," Kara added. "Although they're technically fairy creatures."

"Unbelievable." Ozzie whistled. "So what kind are these?"

Zach shrugged. "I don't know."

"Sea dragons," Marlin said without hesitation.

The healer froze. In all the excitement, it hadn't occurred to her that the magic of the Crystal Caves—

the magic she was supposed to use to heal the water—was contained in these dragon eggs. But how could she just take magic away from these innocent creatures?

"Okay, everyone give Emily some room," Kara instructed. "Let's get this show on the road."

"I can't."

Her friends stared at her, confused.

"Isn't there enough magic?" Lorren asked.

"Plenty, but"—she looked into the merprince's dark brown eyes—"Marlin, if we take it, we risk harming the eggs."

Marlin nodded ruefully. "She's right."

"Then how are we supposed to heal the water?" Kara asked.

"I don't know." Emily bowed her head. "I can't take this magic."

"But I can." A steely voice echoed through the cave.

Everyone whirled.

At the cave's entrance, a shimmer appeared in the shadows. Eyes gleaming beneath her hood, a tall figure strode into the cavern.

"Miranda!" Emily gasped.

"That's far enough!" The warrior was already in fighting stance, wolf stone raised and sparking. Dreamer growled at her side.

Lyra hunched low in front of the other mages, ready to strike.

Miranda paused, surveying the cave. "Impressive."

"Who are you?" Adriane demanded.

"As I told the healer, I am a wizard." She covered her eyes with the back of her hand as Kara shone blazing sunlight over her. The woman's features warped under the strong magic, then flickered back.

"What did you do to me?" Emily demanded, Indi close by her side.

"Looks like I gave you what you wanted," Miranda said, glancing at the unicorn. "Bonding with animals does have its uses." Her hungry eyes fixed on the eggs.

Emily's stomach twisted. "You used me to find this place."

"Consider it a fair exchange."

Adriane fired a warning over the woman's head. The silver bolt hit the crystal wall, showering fragments over the floor. "Who are you, what do you want?"

"Careful, girls," the wizard sneered.

"AgA!" Ozzie cried out. "The eggs!"

Emily whirled around. Jagged cracks ran over several eggs.

"They're hypersensitive to magic," Zach explained, carefully running his palm over a few.

"Adriane. Stop!" Emily commanded.

The warrior lowered her jewel, eyes still locked on the stranger. "How did you get in here?"

"The same way you did."

"Oh, and we just didn't notice you tagging along?" Kara challenged.

"Precisely." Miranda smiled. "Tell them, Emily, how easy it is to make people see what you want them to see."

Kara and Adriane looked at the healer questioningly.

"That doesn't explain how you found us," Emily said coldly.

Miranda held up a small object with blinking lights. "Fascinating device."

Lorren gasped. "Where did you get that?"

"I didn't presume you'd let me just walk in and take this magic." Miranda raised her slender hand. "So I brought along a little insurance."

With a flick of her wrist, the air beside her shimmered, revealing a second figure.

"Tasha!" Lorren cried.

The goblin girl stared blankly into space.

"Let her go!" Kara raised her unicorn jewel.

Miranda shoved the entranced Tasha between herself and the mages. "I don't think so."

Tasha whimpered in pain as sparks flared around her. Kara lowered her gem, unable to get a clear shot at the wizard.

"That's better. Now step away from the eggs," Miranda instructed.

"I don't know who you really are," Emily said, "but a real mage would protect this magic."

"So the Fairimentals can use it?" The woman's cat-like eyes glittered dangerously. "It's only fair I take something *they* want."

"You don't expect us to believe the magic we released from Avalon was *your* magic?" Adriane asked.

The woman eyed the mages. "I used to be like you: a mage with friends, animals, and jewels. My friends betrayed me. The Fairimentals stole my magic and left me with nothing. I taught myself how to be a magic master, a wizard. Now I take magic as I please." Her gaze shifted to Emily. "Just like I showed you."

"You're not taking *this* magic!" Adriane shouted defiantly.

"You didn't seem to mind taking magic from me, warrior. Or have you already forgotten my gift?"

"I've never even seen you before."

"Not in this face, perhaps." Her features blurred, softened.

Miranda tossed back her hood. A jagged white streak zigzagged in her long brown hair. It shimmered into gleaming silver. Her suddenly bloodred lips curled, revealing vampire teeth. Green animal eyes glittered. The Dark Sorceress stepped forward.

"You!" Emily stepped back, horrified.

Adriane and Kara instinctively raised their jewels. Dreamer and Lyra sprang into position.

"Easy, girls." The Dark Sorceress held Tasha

closer. "We're on the same side, you know. It's a shame you can't see that. Soon, it will be too late."

"Never," Emily said between clenched teeth.

"We both want to stop the Spider Witch from reweaving the web, yes?"

"She's next on our list of worst-dressed villains," Kara said.

"Everything I told you was true, healer," the sorceress said smoothly. "My friends and I spent years accumulating magic, storing it in nine crystals. But the Fairimentals hid them. They planned it so only someone with two fairy maps and a powerful unicorn could find the crystals. Then they waited—for you."

Emily was shocked. Why hadn't the Fairimentals told them this?

"What happened to your friends, the other mages?" Zach demanded, keenly interested.

The sorceress stared intently at the blond-haired teen. "Like your parents?"

"You knew my parents?" Zach asked, astonished.

"Tragic, really. When the Fairimentals stole the nine crystals, mage turned against mage." Her slitted gaze flickered to Adriane and Kara, then back to Zach. "Your parents, well . . . once you develop a taste for magic, it's never enough. They were the first to turn to the darker arts."

"You're lying!" Zach cried, a red bolt flaring from his jewel.

Adriane held the boy back. "Don't listen to her."

"What I tell you is true. For years, I have tried to replace what was stolen from me."

"You took magic from the animals and you released Black Fire!" Emily's cheeks flushed with anger as she remembered the horrific damage the sorceress had done. Unable to contain her twisted magic, the Dark Sorceress unleashed a fallout of deadly poison called Black Fire.

"Yes, an unfortunate side effect," the sorceress said.

"You almost killed the mistwolves," Adriane growled.

The sorceress shrugged. "That's magic under the bridge. If the Spider Witch reweaves the web, *all* the magic will be hers. None of us wants that."

Then she turned to Emily, eyes gleaming. "I helped you, healer. Know this. Your power for weaving magic surpasses even hers."

"Say whatever you want." Emily's eyes flared. "You're not getting these eggs."

"I can't fight you alone," the sorceress sighed.

"You got that right!" Adriane snarled.

The Dark Sorceress smiled evilly. "Level Two, you may be, but you're still only mages." She raised her hands, magic flickering from her fingertips. "I have powers you've never dreamed of."

Droplets condensed, covering the crystal walls in a watery sheen. The girls' reflections distorted and multiplied as if they were inside a house of mirrors.

The cave suddenly shook with a loud rumble.

"Criminy!" Cribby dove behind the pile of eggs.

Warily, the mages held their magic in check as the sorceress backed away, Tasha in tow.

Without warning, a surge of water crashed through the cave entrance, flooding across the floor. Red magic sparked from the sorceress's raised hands and the water rose, spinning into a towering cyclone.

"With enough of my power crystals in the Fairimentals' hands, I only needed a magical boost, which the healer was kind enough to provide in our short time together."

The sorceress waved her hands. The tower of water twisted together, forming a bulky figure. Sculpted by dark magic, a terrifying beast came to life, limbs rippling from the water itself. With a thunderous roar, a dozen hissing snake-heads sprouted from its body.

"Crimawager!" Cribby screamed.

"What is that?" Lorren shouted.

The enormous monster heaved forward. Its multiple sinewy necks looped through the air, heading straight toward the mages.

"It's a hydra," Marlin gasped.

"You have done well, mages," the hydra hissed.

The mages exchanged panicked glances.

"Marina!" Emily cried.

The hydra's voice belonged to the missing water Fairimental! Marina was being controlled by the

Dark Sorceress. That's what had twisted all the water magic, not a power crystal. Unwittingly, Emily had strengthened the sorceress by providing her a source of magic.

Lightning fast, the writhing snake-heads swept over the mages and struck like vipers.

"No!" Emily cried out in pain as two eggs shattered, their brittle shells hurling across the cavern.

Glowing magic matter funneled down the hydra's throats, collecting in its thick, clear body. Faint screams echoed along the walls as the life was taken from the baby dragons. As the magic drained into the monster's stomach, its vibrant colors warped into bloodred.

The Dark Sorceress laughed. "The magic will be mine!"

Chapter 15

Jewel fire exploded in the cave. Red, silver, pink, and orange beams ricocheted everywhere as the mages rocketed into action.

Adriane somersaulted through the air and hit the ground in perfect fighting formation, Dreamer snarling beside her. Wolf fire sprang from her stone, slicing through one of the hydra necks. The hissing head splashed to the floor.

"My turn." Kara twirled, blond hair spinning around her. She landed in a crouch, Lyra by her side. Diamond red and white fire ripped through another hydra neck, sending a torrent of water across the cave.

The blazing star smiled at the warrior.

But her triumph was premature.

The severed necks sparked and split apart, sprouting *four* heads where two had been before.

Adriane lashed out again, but only made it worse. The hydra grew two heads for each one the mages lopped off.

"You have to take magic to survive." The sorcer-

ess's raised hands controlled the hydra like a mario-
nette. "I learned that a long time ago."

Tasha stood spellbound beside the sorceress,
unable to move as magic fire sparked dangerously all
around her. Lorren held Kara's gaze for an instant
before disappearing into the shadows at the back of
the cave.

Like twisting serpents, the regenerated heads
latched on to the eggs. Bright magic pulsed down the
hydra's throats.

"Marina!" The healer reached out, desperately
seeking the core of the watermental's magic. "Stop it,
you're killing them!"

A violent flash of deep red sent her reeling back,
heart pounding. Marina was gone, twisted beyond
recognition.

"The magic is mine, one way or another," the sorceress taunted them.

"Save the eggs!" Marlin cried, grabbing two of the
fragile eggs in the nick of time. Two snake-heads
missed by inches, smashing into the floor instead.

"Shield!" Adriane ordered. Warrior and mistwolf
streaked silver fire in a crisscrossing pattern across
the cave.

Kara and Lyra were a step behind them, binding
unicorn power into the shield.

It didn't work. Just as before, wolf and unicorn
power repelled each other, unable to meld.

"Zach!" Adriane yelled.

The boy added blazing dragon fire, binding Kara and Adriane's magic into a shimmering dome. The three threw their shield, blanketing a large pile of eggs. The snake-heads hissed steam, weaving in the air, looking for an opening.

"Go, go, go!" the warrior ordered. "Get the others!"

Emily and Marlin scrambled to rescue the defenseless eggs, depositing them under the protective shield.

"Save the booty!" Cribby yelled as he and Ozzie rolled a large egg behind the mages.

Indi used his nose to roll several eggs out of harm's way.

Arms ablaze with energy, the sorceress furiously pushed the water hydra forward.

Red lightning spiked along the force field as the monster struck. The shield wavered but snapped back in place.

"Give it up!" Kara yelled.

"Keep it coming!" Adriane held her hand palm up, beckoning the sorceress closer, black eyes sparking with fury. "We're going to kick your—"

"Assuming we can hold it," Ozzie fretted, dashing back and forth, depositing eggs in the pile. "We can't stay here forever!"

From the corner of her eye, Emily caught Lorren sneaking along the back of the cave toward Tasha.

"Adriane, keep her distracted." Kara shot a telepathic message to the warrior.

"I thought I was doing that," the warrior replied.

"Oh, good job."

Adriane and Dreamer fired powerful bolts of silver directly at the sorceress, sending her flying against the opposite wall. The magic meter tumbled across the cave floor.

"Distracting enough?"

Kara gave the warrior a thumbs-up.

The sorceress's eyes flared with rage as she got to her feet. Rearing up, the hydra struck again, furiously pounding away at the shield.

Adriane flicked her wrist. Easily sidestepping the lumbering hydra, Dreamer lunged at the enemy.

The Dark Sorceress spun and fired at the mistwolf—only to hit bare crystal walls. Dreamer had vanished, leaving a trail of misty sparkles.

"That's all the eggs," Ozzie announced, patting his forehead with a paw.

Emily frantically surveyed the pile beneath the glowing shield. There were hundreds. What was she going to do now?

"Huddle up," Adriane ordered.

"What's the plan?" Kara asked as the mages gathered behind the dome.

The warrior turned to Emily. "What about it, Doc?"

"Marina is the cause of the water sickness." Emily was thinking aloud. "We can't heal the water unless we heal her."

"The Dark Sorceress gave us the fourth power crystal," the warrior said. "I bet it was tainted."

"They all could have been tainted," Ozzie said. "She claims they were her crystals to begin with."

"Can you heal Marina?" Marlin asked Emily, eyes wide with fear.

"I can't use this magic," Emily said, glancing at the eggs. "It would destroy them."

"We can't keep this up," Zach reminded them as the hydra battered the shield. "Something's got to give."

As if on cue, several eggs began to shudder and crack.

Marlin's face flushed. "What's happening to them?"

"Too much magical energy," Zach cried. "They're starting to hatch!"

"Do something!" Marlin screamed.

"What am I supposed to do?" Emily cried.

Large cracks began spreading over dozens of eggs.

"We can't let them hatch," Zach called out. "They'll imprint on the first person they see."

"I'm calling Starfire," Kara announced, preparing to summon her paladin, the fire stallion. "He can help us heal Marina."

"I'm calling Stormbringer." The warrior raised her wolf stone.

"We can't risk using your paladins!" Emily cried. "Their magic is too strong. All these eggs would hatch!"

"Everyone, calm down!" Ozzie ordered as six eggs shuddered, cracking open in front of his eyes. "GaH!" the ferret screamed and ran around in circles. "Help!"

Emily felt the world close in around her. Ragged breath caught in her throat as she fought to stay calm.

"Time," the healer said, spinning to face Zach. "We need time. That's your department."

"I'll try." Zach closed his eyes, dragon stone glowing as he called upon his elemental power of time. Sweat broke on his brow as rings of magic pulsed weakly from his wrist, trickling over the mages.

"Hurry up!" the blazing star ordered.

"Careful, Zach," Adriane cautioned.

"Oh, give me that magic." Kara swung her jewel, locking unicorn power around Zach's wrist. The boy cried out as Kara seized his magic, forcing it over the eggs and encircling the hydra.

"Kara, stop!" In a blaze of silver, Adriane tried to fight Kara off.

But the blazing star's magic was unstoppable. It latched on to the wolf stone, too! Kara's magic was greedy, hungry, consuming everything in its path. The shield crackled with the impact, threatening to rip to pieces.

"Kara, let go!" Emily grabbed Kara's arm, trying to pull her back. With Lyra helping her, they pulled Kara and Zach apart.

"What are you doing?" Zach yelled, rubbing his arms.

Kara fell back. "What does it look like? I'm saving the eggs."

"You're out of control!" Adriane shouted.

Lyra stepped in front of Kara protectively, teeth bared.

"Stop it!" Ozzie bellowed as he planted himself between the two mages.

Kara and Adriane glared at each other, jewels pulsing dangerously.

"We have enough to deal with without you two going at it!"

But Kara's boost had worked. Zach's time magic had slowed the hydra, its dozens of necks bobbing and weaving sluggishly. Even the Dark Sorceress seemed unable to lift her arms to control the water-mental.

"Kara, you can't just take magic like that," Emily exclaimed.

"I was only helping." The blazing star sneered at Adriane.

"You hurt him!" the warrior snarled.

"I'm fine, just keep sending me power," Zach said evenly, stone sparking as his time magic held the hydra at bay.

"Okay," Ozzie squeaked, lying over three eggs that had rolled free of the shield. "But no more surprises."

Suddenly, Lorren appeared out of thin air, Tasha beside him.

"Ahhh!"

"Tasha!" Kara hugged her, then held her at arm's length. "Are you all right?"

"I think so. Gertie and I landed downriver and the next thing I knew, I was in this cave."

"Sounds like the same spell we were under," Marlin said.

The air sparkled as Dreamer's invisible mist reshaped into solid wolf form. Tasha's magic meter was clamped firmly in his mouth.

"Thanks, Dreamer." Tasha cleaned it with the hem of her robe and started pushing buttons. "Holy cow!"

"*Unicorn,*" Indi corrected her.

"Emily . . ." Ozzie wobbled as an egg beneath him shuddered. The shell fractured as a tiny, webbed fin reached out, struggling to free itself.

The ferret leaped in the air. "It's hatching!"

Emily knelt next to it as Indi watched her with wide eyes. She had so badly wanted a bonded animal, and now it looked like she was going to get her wish tenfold!

"Emily, look out!"

Marlin pushed Emily aside as the infant dragon poked his long nose through the crumbling shell. The baby wailed mournfully, searching for its mother. Large, wet eyes locked on Marlin. With a joyful squeal, the creature sprang into the arms of the merprince. He screamed as they tumbled backward together, vanishing into the pile of eggs.

The cave echoed with the wail of newborns as more eggs began hatching.

Emily felt the familiar tingle of panic. She had to heal Marina before all the eggs hatched. These infants wouldn't have a chance against the virus. But there was no power crystal.

"What are we going to do?" Kara asked.

Her friends looked at her anxiously. Adriane and Kara were tiring; Zach's magic was already fading. Their magic shield wouldn't last.

Emily had no choice: She would have to weave her web again. She needed the magic of *every* water animal to heal Marina. Fear burned through her. What if she lost control like the last time?

It was a risk she had to take.

"I have to try healing Marina," Emily said. "I'm going to need all your help."

"I can't work with *her*." Adriane pointed at Kara.

"Not my fault *my* jewel is so much more powerful," Kara snapped.

"I can guide your frequency levels so they blend together better," Tasha suggested, tweaking her magic meter.

"Okay?" Emily asked Adriane and Kara.

Her friends nodded as magic pulsed from their jewels.

"Zach, keep your magic focused on the eggs," Emily ordered.

"Right." The blond teen nodded.

Adriane and Dreamer stood to Emily's left, silver wolf magic swirling from Adriane's gem.

Kara and Lyra, on the right, released a diamond cloud of sparkly magic.

"Less wolf, more cat." Tasha watched colored lines move up the meter.

Following Tasha's instructions, Adriane, Dreamer, Kara, and Lyra managed to hold their magic in balance.

Emily fought the tightening in her stomach, pushing the fear to a place where she could harness it, use it.

"Indi." She looked at the unicorn eye-to-eye. "I can't do this without you."

Confidence and love shone in his eyes. *"I do good."*

Centering herself, Emily gazed at the colors swirling around the eggs. Reaching her hand around the shield, a tiny spray of the hydra's water washed through her fingers. Droplets covered her silver bracelet, sparkling like diamonds, washed clean by the magic of the sea dragon eggs.

She closed her eyes and concentrated, opening herself to the water magic. She visualized fine lines radiating, then stretching out, leading to every lake, river, and stream, melding with the warm undercurrent flowing in the oceans.

Carefully, she weaved the lines of magic together, forming a delicate web. Feeling the boost of her friends as Tasha carefully monitored her meters, Emily reached out to the animals. Indi balanced her, giving her everything he could to keep her strong.

Lights flared along the web, brilliant points of stars flickering to life.

Drawn to the healing magic, dozens, then hundreds, then thousands of animals came to her. Building in power, their magic thundered down the strands of the healer's magic web.

"Here it comes!" Tasha's jewel meter beeped and whirred.

Arms outstretched, Emily felt the power rush through her. She *connected* with Indi, and knew instinctively where the sickness had struck Marina.

"Now!" she cried.

The magic moved at her command. Rushing from her, it encircled the hydra in a ring of blazing blue fire. With every last ounce of strength, Emily drove healing magic right into the core of the sickness.

The explosion was so intense, Emily almost blacked out. Fire filled every pore of her being as the virus leaped from Marina into the healer. The agonizing pain of every animal she'd summoned seared through her body, suffocating her as if she were drowning.

Then—in a heartbeat—the pain stopped. The hydra convulsed and fell apart, splattering to the floor.

Emily scanned the cave, dazed. Without the hydra to fight for her, The Dark Sorceress had vanished.

"We did it!" Kara shouted, raising her hands.

"That was amazing!" Adriane agreed, high-fiving the blazing star.

Emily struggled to focus as she reached for Indi. What she saw made her gasp. The unicorn's aura pulsed bloodred. He had absorbed the full brunt of the water virus not only from Marina, but from every creature in her vast web.

"No, Indi!"

Shifting patterns of red spiked like fire, refusing to match his shape. The unicorn *wasn't* his true form after all—but what was?

"Unbelievable!" Tasha exclaimed, gripping her glowing magic meter.

"We are so rad," Kara bragged.

"Very cool," Adriane agreed.

"Yes, but I've isolated another jewel frequency," Tasha said, adjusting buttons. "Whoa."

"What is it?" Zach asked.

Tasha looked up. "Power crystal."

Emily's heart skipped a beat.

"Where?" Lorren asked.

"It's . . . right there."

Everyone looked to where Tasha pointed.

"Indi?" The truth hit Emily with stunning clarity. "A power crystal."

She watched in horror as the virus attacked the creature, tearing his magic apart. Indi desperately struggled to hold his form. But he had given everything he had to save her.

"Indi do good, Emilee." Indi's beautiful unicorn body melted away like wax.

"Wait!" she cried, reaching out for him. "Please, don't go!"

The creature that was Indi slipped from her grasp, leaving a faint whisper of profound longing and gratitude—the last, lonely cry of a living, magical animal.

Chapter 16

Gentle waves lapped over white sands. Emily whirled around, taking in the turquoise ocean and swaying palms. Near the treeline, blackened driftwood lay scattered in the ashes of a campfire. She'd been transported back to the island where they'd started. But how? Why?

Behind her, leaves shook faintly.

"Indi?" In the dense tropical foliage, Indi's magical aura flared chaotically, shifting from gold to blue, green, pink, and purple.

"What's happened to you?"

Waves of distress radiated from the bushes.

"I know you're here." Emily took a step closer. "Please come out."

"No."

"Why not?"

"I ugly blob."

"I don't care what you look like."

The spiky colors calmed with her words. Fronds rustled, and a shadowy shape hesitantly emerged.

Emily's breath caught.

The thing before her was horribly misshapen. Indi's unicorn shape had melted into a lumpy gray mass. Patches of pink and purple crystal rippled in irregular patterns over his body. Fuzzy ears stuck out at weird angles, and a long tail dragged behind him as he hobbled across the sand on stubby legs. Only a pair of pained indigo eyes told Emily she was looking at the same creature.

The healer gently placed her hands on Indi's lumpy form, trying to calm him. "Why did you bring us back here?"

"*I* brought you here," a gentle voice said.

Mist rose from the water's edge. Emily could hardly believe her eyes as a form began to take shape from the water itself—the figure of a woman rising from the ocean. Long hair flowed in soft waves down her back, framing a delicate face. A crystalline aura dazzled around her like a diamond cloak.

"Marina?" Emily asked, even though she knew it was not the Fairimental.

Clear azure eyes met Emily's gaze. "I am a water sylph, Neerie, a guardian of Avalon." Her voice was light and melodic, like a mountain stream.

Emily stood awkwardly, unsure what to do. Sylphs were powerful creatures of elemental magic.

"I'm Emily," she blurted out.

"I know who you are, young healer." The sylph

glided across the water like a shimmering angel. "I have been waiting for the heart."

"The heart?"

"The Heart of Avalon." She gestured to the shivering mass beside Emily. "The most powerful of the nine crystals."

"Pretty unicorn," Indi protested weakly.

"Why do you resist your true form?" the sylph asked, eyes shining.

"I am for Emilee." Indi's voice trembled.

Crystalline facets began to spread over his molten torso but still he struggled to keep the unicorn shape.

"A power crystal wanted to become a real animal for me?" Emily said shyly, then frowned at Neerie. "Why didn't you just take him when we first got here?"

"The Heart of Avalon needed to be charged with the purest of magic. Only by becoming a true bonded could he transform."

"Why can't he stay a unicorn?" Emily asked.

"That is impossible. He is a power crystal designed to strengthen all the magic of Avalon."

And suddenly, Emily got it: Power crystals were drawn to magic. But Indi had been drawn to Emily because, inside, he needed pure magic to survive. And the purest magic came from the bond between humans and animals. During their journey, he'd learned what he needed most: that true magic could not be taken, but must be given freely. Indi had sacrificed himself to save her from the virus and now, Emily realized, each would have to make the most painful sacrifice of all.

The sylph reached a gleaming hand toward Indi. "It is time to come home."

Indi moved toward Emily. *"You stay with me, Emily."*

"I wish I could." Emily's throat tightened with tears.

Indi shivered, clinging with lumpy paws. *"I be good."*

"I know." Kneeling, she gazed into Indi's deep blue eyes. Instantly, she felt the amazing magic inside. But it was tinged with deep loneliness. All he wanted was to be a real animal and stay with her.

"Indi, you must go back." Emily hugged the creature, rocking him gently. No matter what he was, their connection was deep and real. "You have to be who you really are."

"I not pretty unicorn."

Emily could feel the sorrow pouring from him as Indi finally resigned himself to his fate. With a shuddering sigh, all the color washed away as the creature that was Indi began to shrink, folding in on itself, shapeshifting for the last time. In her outstretched hands, Emily held a plain gray, heart-shaped rock.

"You don't love me anymore."

"No," Emily stammered. "That's not what I meant."

With a loud crack, the stone split down the middle.

"Indi!" Emily sank to her knees, aghast.

Two halves fell to the sand like tears, two pieces of a broken heart. Emily frantically searched for Indi's bright aura. "I can't see his magic!"

"The heart is gone." Neerie bowed her head. Water streamed from her body as if every part of her cried.

Emily gazed up at Neerie. No shining lights appeared around the water sylph, either. Without Indi, she couldn't see magic anymore! It was as if she were right back where she'd started. And this time she had no jewel to help her. Worst of all, she had lost her bonded.

"How do I heal him?" she pleaded.

"All that he has become is still there, if you look into your own heart," counseled Neerie.

Emily pictured Indi, a beautiful unicorn prancing proudly about the deck of the Fearless Flyer. A tear slipped down her cheek as she remembered the pure joy he had felt being her magical animal.

She gazed at her empty silver bracelet. She could do this—she had to. Closing her eyes, she reached for Indi's magic. A familiar flicker of blue light tickled at her senses, her jewel, buried deep in the heart.

Gathering her courage, she picked up the two halves of Indi's broken heart and gazed deep into the gray rock. A little pink and purple aura sparked faintly, like a tiny flame.

She gently weaved the cool blues and greens of her own magic around his. Emily felt her magic inside him, a part of him now, sustaining him. It was time to let her jewel go. "You never have to be lonely again."

"Stuck."

"Always."

With the full force of her magic, she brought the two halves together.

The two auras swirled into one glittering rainbow, a perfect match, like two pieces of a puzzle. In a bright flash, crystalline facets sparkled around the dull gray rock, transforming it into a dazzling heart-shaped crystal.

It was the most beautiful jewel she had ever seen.

"My magic healed him," Emily cried happily.

The vibrant power crystal floated into Neerie's outstretched hands. "The strength of your love healed the heart."

From inside the crystal, Indi's reflection looked at Emily with bright indigo eyes. She could see Indi's magic glowing stronger than ever. But this time, his aura fit his shape. This was who he truly was. A power crystal—the Heart of Avalon.

"I'll miss you." Emily smiled, steeling herself against the pain of losing her bonded. "You are every-thing that I wanted." Hands covering her face, the healer wept.

Light blazed from the heart's center as the power crystal released its true magic. Swirling like crystal rain, Indi's bright aura cascaded over her, washing away the pain. Emily opened her eyes in wonder as the twinkling magic merged into the shape of a large, four-legged creature.

"Indi!" Emily exclaimed.

As the light faded, Indi stood in front of her. He was no longer a colt, but a full-grown unicorn stallion.

Surprised, Indi looked himself over, stamping glittering magic from long, muscled legs. His hide swirled in deep purples and pinks, and his crystal horn gleamed with all the colors of the rainbow.

"I bigger, better than ever unicorn!"

The sylph's eyes twinkled. "He has bonded with you in the only way he could. He has chosen to be your paladin, if you will accept him."

"I do." Emily threw her arms around the unicorn's neck. Her paladin. She was a Level Two mage. "I love you, Indi."

The sylph smiled sweetly. "A unicorn can give its magic to whomever he chooses."

In a brilliant flash, a gem appeared in Emily's open hand. But it was not the familiar blues and greens of her original healing stone that shone forth. Dancing patterns of red, yellow, gold, silver, all the colors of the rainbow, filled her transformed jewel.

"Thank you," Emily beamed as she fastened it

back onto her silver bracelet. "I thought I might never bond with an animal."

"Healer, you are not meant to bond with an animal," Neerie told her.

Emily's heart sank. It always seemed to come to this moment: She would get so close with an animal only to be left alone in the end.

"You've taught the heart the true meaning of magic—the love between mage and bonded. Your gift is to strengthen that bond between all humans and animals. The way you have bonded with Indi."

Realization hit Emily like a bolt of lightning: the dragon eggs. They were the hope of Aldenmor's water magic. Suddenly she knew what she needed to do—what she was meant to do.

"This is your destiny, healer." Neerie smiled at her. "Make the magic new again."

Emily wanted to jump up and down in excitement. Her jewel had evolved. She had reached Level Two and she had her paladin to help her when she needed him. Forever.

"What about the heart?" Emily asked, gazing at the crystal shining in Neerie's hands.

"When you have retrieved all the crystals, you must bring them back here. The Heart of Avalon will remain to show you the way."

Emily climbed onto Indi's back, sitting proudly atop her paladin. "We need to get back to our friends."

The unicorn shook his magnificent head and long purple mane. Whirling around, his hooves kicked up glittering stardust. Magic swirled from his horn, opening a dazzling rainbow portal. Rearing up on his hind legs, Indi prepared to jump.

Holding the heart high above her head, Neerie began to melt back into the crystal clear waters.

"Wait." Emily turned to the sylph. "Where *is* Avalon?"

Sweet as summer rain, the sylph spoke. "Avalon is where your heart is."

Chapter 17

The sound of steel drums and clamshell cas-
tanets fell silent as Marlin held up his hand.
Everyone turned toward the stage.

"I am Prince Marlin, heir to the throne of Aquatania," he said, voice booming over the crowd.

Standing on a raised podium just off the shores of
Aquatania Beach, he looked every inch the prince,
dressed in red velvet robes dotted with golden jewels.
The domes of the city spread behind him, glittering in
the surf. His father, King Spartos, sat beside him,
scanning the representatives from Aldenmor gathered to hear the prince's speech.

"This year, the Wave Fest is truly a special celebra-
tion," Marlin continued, gesturing across the beach.
"Today we are making magic."

Anxious merboys and girls formed a long line,
waiting. And at the front stood Emily, Ozzie, and the
other mages. Beside them a pile of dazzling eggs
shone with all the colors of the rainbow.

"What is the meaning of this?" King Spartos

rose to his feet as startled gasps ran through the crowd.

"Father, you have taught me the rich history of the merfolk," Marlin said. "But a future without magic is a future *without* merfolk."

"You promise something you cannot deliver," the king said, regarding his son sternly. "We must face the truth."

"This *is* our truth," Marlin's voice rang out. "We must not, cannot let magic die!"

Jaaran, Kee-lyn, and the other dragon riders applauded.

King Spartos nodded curtly, not convinced, but willing to give his son a chance.

Marlin sought out Emily and smiled, confidence shining in his eyes.

The healer took a deep breath as hundreds of anxious eyes turned to her. She gestured to the first merboy in line: a skinny teenager with dark curls, and black eyes wide with fear and excitement. He approached Emily and knelt in the sand.

Concentrating, she saw his magical aura dancing around him, pure and bright as a sunrise. Her rainbow jewel sparkled in the same colors.

With the strength of her paladin, she sent golden light shimmering over the eggs, searching for the perfect match. And then, from deep in the pile, an aura glinted. The magic was strong, its bright pattern about the same size, shape, and luminance as the boy's—a perfect magical fit. Biting her lip, she carefully extracted a yellow-gold egg and placed it before the merboy.

The entire crowd took a collective breath as a loud crack echoed up and down the beach. A crooning noise filled the air as a small fin pushed a section of shell away. An infant sea dragon suddenly popped his head out, eyes blinking in wonder. The merboy reached with trembling hands, peeling the sticky shell from the baby's head. Wide eyes locked together.

Emily alone could see their bright auras float together, blending into a bright new golden pattern filled with hope and promise.

With a squeal of joy, the baby dragon flopped into the waiting arms of its bonded. The boy rose to his feet, holding his new friend aloft. The crowd erupted in cheers as the other teens congratulated the boy, eagerly waiting for their chance to get their own bonded dragon.

"Remarkable," King Spartos exclaimed as he surveyed the ecstatic crowd. Then he turned to the prince. "I applaud the prince and the mages for this gift. But, son, how did you know they would bond?"

"I am the merfolk prince." Marlin met his father's gaze. "But I am also a dragon rider."

The merprince shook off his ceremonial robe, revealing a blue-green jumpsuit underneath, the traditional garb of the dragon riders. Shock registered on the faces of the king and the merfolk in the crowd.

Marlin waved a hand toward the water. "I bring you—my bonded, Niva."

Scales of purple and green glittered over Niva's sleek body as she rose from the waters. Marlin dove in to meet her. In an instant, he resurfaced astride the beautiful sea dragon's back.

"And . . . Harry, Elroy, Avril, Bertrum, Fizzles—well . . . you'll meet them all later."

A dozen baby dragons frolicked around Niva, adoring eyes locked on Marlin.

Niva reared up in the waves as the merprince raised his fist in the air triumphantly. "Together we will spread our magic throughout the oceans, and all of Aldenmor—for what once was, and for what will be again!"

Jaaran and Kee-lyn stepped forward and clapped, joined by the other riders. Soon everyone at the Wave Fest was cheering wildly at the prince's proclamation.

Off shore, the sea dragons of Aquatania leaped into the air, scales gleaming as they splashed happily in the water. The merprince grinned ear to ear as Niva deposited him on the beach by the eggs, six baby sea dragons bundled in his arms. Several more clung to his legs and feet.

Joy filled Emily as she saw Marlin's magical aura, clear and bright. Niva and a dozen babies had increased his magic tenfold.

From the waves, a figure made of water surged to the surface. Flowing aquamarine hair highlighted with turquoise danced on the frothy spray.

"Marina!" Emily cried.

"The sea dragons will keep the water magic strong," the shimmering blue watermental said, smiling. "Thank you, all."

Kara stepped forward. "What about the other crystals in the Jewel Keep?"

"Are they tainted?" Lorren asked.

"When the heart was awakened, the other crystals were healed as well," the Fairimental explained.

"Was the Dark Sorceress really once a mage?" Kara asked.

"That is true, blazing star," Marina admitted.

"Did you take the power crystals from her?" Emily asked.

"No. Beings more powerful than us, the Guardians of Avalon, took the crystals to a hidden island."

"So was it the sorceress's magic?" Adriane asked.

Marina continued. "The Dark Sorceress and her allies stored strong magic in nine crystals. The crystals were taken before they could be turned against us. The Guardians allowed you to release that magic to save Aldenmor but the power crystals were wiped clean. They could be tuned either way, for good or evil."

Emily nodded. "That's how you became twisted. The sorceress planned it all along."

"Do the sorceress and Spider Witch know of these Guardians?" Adriane asked.

"They have remained hidden, protecting places of magic along the web."

"Like the forest sylph of Ravenswood," Adriane mused.

Marina nodded. "The Guardians wait for you to return the crystals."

Emily thought of Neerie, the water sylph, waiting for her to bring back the heart. If the Dark Sorceress and Spider Witch didn't know about these Guardians, maybe the mages had a chance after all.

"Who made the power crystals?" Kara asked.

"That remains a mystery," Marina said.

"At least we know where to bring the crystals when we have them," Marlin said, and smiled at Emily.

Marina flowed over the water. "We know that, long ago, the sorceress and her allies tried to open the gates to Avalon. We believe that hidden island is the same gateway. It falls upon you, mages, to succeed where they failed."

Emily and Marlin exchanged a startled glance. Had they really been at the gateway to Avalon?

"We'll find the other crystals," Tasha exclaimed, proudly displaying her magic meter.

"All right, who's next?" Ozzie stomped up and down the line of waiting merteens, clam-on-a-stick held behind his back. Two of Marlin's baby dragons waddled after him and gobbled up the treat. The ferret turned and bit down on a wooden twig.

"Who's a good widdie biddie dragon?"

"Cribby?" Emily turned incredulously.

The ornery sea elf sat in the sand, cradling a white and gold sea dragon pup in his arms. Cribby tickled the happy pup, then looked up at Emily. "What? So the merboy missed one."

Marlin grinned. "Looks like you have a new first matey."

With a toothy smile, Cribby held the wide-eyed pup over his head. "His name's Cribby, Jr."

"Wonderful." Emily beamed. "Good job, Cribby . . . and Cribby, Jr."

"Can I pick one out?" Kara was practically dancing. "Come on, Em, pleeeeeeze!"

"Sure, everyone can." Emily smiled. "Show them to me as each rider approaches. I'll know if it's the right match."

"All right!"

Lorren, Kara, and Tasha fell into the eggs like kids on Christmas morning.

Jaaran approached the merprince, Kee-lyn by his side. "Marlin, I'm sorry." The tall rider spoke without hesitation or embarrassment. "We were wrong about you."

"No, it's me who should be sorry." Marlin faced the warrior squarely.

"You saved the dragons and our magic." Gratitude shone from Kee-lyn's eyes.

"Believe me, I had a lot of help." He gestured toward Emily and the mages.

Kee-lyn smiled at the healer. "We'll have our hands full training the new riders and dragons."

"We all have important work to do now, keeping the magic strong. We want you to know, Marlin, the dragon riders swear their allegiance to the future king of Aquatania." Jaaran extended his hand.

Marlin grasped it firmly. Jaaran and Kee-lyn nodded, then left to join the others by the eggs.

Marlin gazed at Emily shyly. "Still have some things to work out with my father, you know. I guess that's how it is."

"You stood up for what you believe in. He has to respect that." She gazed at the king, proudly accepting congratulations from the guests. "I think he knows how lucky Aquatania is to have a prince like you."

He took her hand in his and looked deeply into her eyes. "No one ever saw magic in me, until you."

Emily blushed bright red.

"How's this one?" Kara plopped a bright orange and yellow egg in Marlin's hands.

"Kara." Emily giggled as the blazing star winked at her.

"I need to Google you." The blazing matchmaker

pulled the befuddled prince away, leaving Emily alone. "See how you match up with our healer."

Turning, the healer spotted a solitary figure watching the ocean, her back to the happy throngs. The tall warrior's magic shone like a full moon in the midnight sky, full of mystery, deep as the night. Emily strode over to her.

Adriane turned and smiled. "Good work, Doc."

"Thanks." Emily looked around. "Where's Zach and Drake?"

"They left to find Moonshadow and the mist-wolves. He still has a lot of questions about his parents," Adriane said, then asked abruptly: "Have you noticed anything different about Kara?"

"You mean she's pushier than normal?" Emily joked, but she could feel the anger radiating from the warrior's tense figure.

"You just can't force others to use their magic." Adriane's dark eyes shifted toward Kara distrustfully. "She could've really hurt Zach."

"Adriane, she didn't mean to do that," Emily said gently. "In the heat of the moment, she was just trying to help."

"That wasn't the first time she's lost control of her magic," Adriane said coolly. "And it won't be the last."

A chill went up Emily's back.

"This one!"

"No, this one!"

"Emily, come on! Which one?"

"GaH!" Ozzie dashed by, clutching an egg as the dragon riders chased him.

"Hey," the healer said, smiling at Adriane. "Come help with the eggs. It's so much fun—"

"No, I'm going to take a run. Later."

Emily sighed. Ever since the Crystal Caves, there'd been a new tension between the warrior and the blazing star. She might be the healer, but she had no idea how to heal the relationship between her two closest friends.

She watched Adriane jog down the beach. As if from thin air, Dreamer appeared by her side, easily keeping stride with the warrior's fast pace. Emily blinked, startled by the silver magic glowing in a perfect halo between them. Instead of two individual patterns blended together, their aura was one solid circle, as if they were one and the same.

She turned her gaze to Kara. The blond teen sparkled with beauty as she chitchatted with Lorren, Marlin, Tasha, and King Spartos. Adriane's magic might be shadowy and mysterious, but Kara's magic could blind you.

Emily knew Kara had a good heart, but she did share some of Adriane's concern. The blazing star was meant to enhance magic, but if she wasn't careful, her brilliance would eclipse everyone around her.

And what about her own healing magic? Being a Level Two mage seemed to only offer more questions than answers. What did it really mean to weave magic? Was she really as powerful as the Spider Witch?

She thought of the mermaid's dark predictions. The healer *had* experienced a darker side of her powers, just as Kara and Adriane had in the past. Maybe the mermaids had only sensed Emily's fear—or maybe they were right.

One thing was certain: They had all been changed by the magic. Each of the mages was stronger than she'd ever been before. But using stronger magic meant greater risks, for all of them.

How much would they change in their quest for magic? Could the mages stand strong, together, to face the challenges ahead? Or would they be pulled apart?

Emily gazed out at the hopeful faces of the dragon riders and her friends, all waiting for the touch of a healer.

She'd be busy the rest of the afternoon matching teens with their bonded dragons, and she couldn't be more thrilled. Thanks to Indi, Emily understood that the heart of all magic came from that friendship between animals and humans.

She smiled. Indi could never be a real animal. But, in the end, by choosing to be his true self, he had only become stronger. And in so doing, he had helped Emily choose to accept the truth about her magic.

She was a healer.

And if it hurt to love so much, that was the price she had to pay.

Epilogue

"**B**e careful with those!" the Dark Sorceress yelled as she strode through the courtyard behind her new keep.

Oxen stamped and snorted, terrified, as several orcs edged giant cages off a flatbed cart.

One of the cages dropped hard, releasing a blood-curdling shriek.

The sorceress peered through the glowing bars. The cage seemed empty, but she knew better.

Phantom wraiths were invisible without the right magic to see them. Magic eaters, especially vicious ones at that, phantom wraiths lived in the Other-worlds and were very hard to trap. But the healer's web attracted magical animals—all kinds of animals.

"Easy, my pets." The sorceress smiled, and then turned to the orcs. "Put them with the others."

"Yes, mistress." The orc bowed.

She continued through the teeming courtyard where imps, goblins, and trolls worked by torchlight, erecting a spiked barrier encircling the stone towers of the keep. While the Fairimentals planted daisies in the ruins of her former lair, she was creating an impenetrable stronghold.

All was going according to plan.

The Dark Sorceress flung open a set of heavy wooden doors and swept into her new lair, red lips curved in a satisfied smile. The workers she had found in Port Tuga had done well, quickly constructing this magnificent keep hidden in the Black Woods. A group of lizard-like servants froze as she passed by them, and then hurriedly continued laying the black marble floors. The entire chamber gleamed, setting off her ornate silver throne. A fitting place from which to rule the magic web.

She turned down a long hallway, relishing the spacious chambers opening on either side. A definite improvement over her lair in the Shadowlands, and far superior to the Spider Witch's moldering castle.

Cold fire flared inside her. The Spider Witch was moving fast. Soon, her former ally would control another key point of magic, and be one step closer to reweaving the magic web. The sorceress could not let that happen.

The mages believed they had defeated her in the Crystal Caves, as she had intended. Let them think she was weak—that would only work to her advantage. Securing the magic of the dragon eggs would have been nice, but it would *all* be hers soon enough. Until then, the magic she had tricked the healer into acquiring would do quite nicely.

Entering the room at the end of the hallway, she moved to the seeing pool set in the polished black floor. Reflections from the water sent patterns of light dancing across the walls.

The mages were powerful—Level Two now. But she knew better than anyone that the more magic that one used, the more one needed to fill the hole left inside. That could be turned against them.

She smiled, vampire teeth glinting. She had touched the redheaded healer's mind and tested her abilities to weave magic with astounding results. It shouldn't have been a surprise. After all, the Spider Witch had once been a healer herself.

If Avalon truly existed, as the Fairimentals believed, then she could not risk that power falling into the Spider Witch's web. And if these mages were destined to open the gates of Avalon, she had to get the rest of the crystals into their hands, and fast.

With a long claw, she swirled the pool's dark water thoughtfully. It was unexpected that one of the power crystals had turned into a living creature. Even a magic master like her could not predict what such concentrations of animal magic would do.

One thing she knew for certain. When the mages discovered the secrets of the remaining crystals, they were going to wish they had never gotten involved with magic. Only the wizard that designed them would know how to control their powers.

With a sweep of her arm, she conjured her dark

magic. The seeing pool shimmered in colors as the air warped. Reaching into the dream state, she lashed out, taking control of the one who would serve her.

❧　　❧　　❧

Across time and space, in another world, Henry Gardener awoke with a start, eyes blazing red. Shackled in his prison of black ice, the wizard rose to his feet. Every joint in his body ached from his spellbound slumber.

"It is time," a cold voice sliced through his mind. "I have need of you, old friend."

The World of

AvALon

Friends Forever Tee Shirt

The Friends Forever Tee Shirt is a great way to share the magic of Avalon. The Tee Shirt is printed in FULL COLOR. It is made of 4.2 ounce combed ring-spun semi-sheer cotton. It has a contrast neck and raglan sleeves. Sizes S-M-L-XL (see chart)

Colors Body/Sleeves & Collar
1382-P   White/Frost Pink
1382-B   White/Frost Sky

$14.95
Plus S&H

SIMPLE SIZE GUIDE

	S	M	L	XL
Length*	20"	22.5"	23.5"	26"
Width**	15"	16"	18"	19"

*Measure from top of shoulder to bottom of hem.
**Measure chest width from arm pit to arm pit.

How to Order:

Visit: www.avalonclubhouse.com
Visit: www. winterpeople.com
Call: 800.552.6199 • Fax: 207.865.6636
Mail: Winter People, Inc.
        125 US Rt 1 • Freeport, ME 04032

Item #	Qty	Size	Color	Price	Total

Shipping Charges:
$4.95/shirt within the continental U.S.
Outside the US, Please call for pricing
800.552.6199.

Subtotal	
Shipping	
TOTAL	

Name _____

Address _____

City_____State _____ Zip _____

Phone _____

Email _____

Method of Payment (please check):
SORRY, NO CASH OR PERSONAL CHECKS
☐ Cashier Check: Payable to Winter People

☐ Credit Card:
    ☐ VISA ☐ MasterCard
    ☐ American Express ☐ Discover Card

Name on Card _____

Acct # _____

Expiration Date (mm/yy)_____ PVV_____

Signature _____